Dedication

For my mother Jean Russell

When we moved to Italy, we had only been in Ohio for 3 months and then Dad got the Italy position. It was my mother who sold the house, put our things in storage, packed for the 5 kids going, got us the necessary immunizations, and countless other tasks and she did it alone while my Dad had gone on ahead to set up the new business there. Her bravery and courage both before and after we moved there knew no boundaries. She is a champion. A hero. I recently learned about our adventure in Italy from her perspective. From the upheaval of our family moving to another country her perseverance paved the way for an unforgettable and enriching experience. I came to deeply respect the life she gave us. She made sure we were cultured by taking us to museums, on tours, and we visited many places like Capri, Sardinia, Sargento, Florence, Pisa, Venice, Sicily and many place both north and south of Rome. These were priceless experiences and she showed us how to handle most situations no matter how tough and do it with grace and dignity. We quickly grew to love the Italian people and culture. While eventually the finances increased, we were at times living on the edge of poverty and mom somehow figured out a way to feed 7 people on almost no money. Mom, you were the woman behind the man. Dad couldn't have done it without you. It was a grand adventure and I want to say thank you for all that you did for our family, not just in Italy, but in life.

Cheers to you Mom, You continue to amaze me.

Love, Jannie

Dreams come true

on

Cedarcrest Lake

Chapter 1

When Kate was a young girl, she lived in a townhouse with her parents. As an only child, she often felt lonely and longed for a sibling that would never come. Her mother worked at the church three days a week. In the summer, Kate would go next door to be cared for by an Italian woman called Dorothea. Dotti, as she was called by Americans. Dotti had come over from northern Italy, after the war, with her American husband, barely speaking a word of English. She was a tiny woman that stood about 4 foot 9 inches and had a beautiful laugh. Kate loved her like a grandmother. Dotti doted on the little girl even though she had five children of her own that were grown and on their own. Dotti introduced Kate to Italian food, culture, and her love for Italy. She brought Kate under her wing in the kitchen and let her stand on a chair as she taught her about Italian cooking. Kate had a hard time understanding her thick accent sometimes, but she learned with her eyes, and she learned with her heart. The magic behind Italian cuisine ,she learned, was love and family. Dotti had shared stories of her life as a girl from Trieste and told her how she used to go out with her mother in the country hills and pick Dandelion greens for salads. Kate had dreamed of Italy since the old woman had passed away 20 years ago and now her dream was coming true!

Kate ran a nervous hand through her long-tangled hair as she watched the suitcases come off the belt in the Leonardo da Vinci airport in Rome. It had been a long, but comfortable, flight from the Twin Cities. Drew had gotten first class flights and they had been able to sleep, watch a movie, and get free food and drinks. Kate had never flown before and this was a great experience. Drew, having been a pilot, was able to get the tickets at a much lower price with his passes as a former pilot. It was an almost 12-hour flight, but it was good because departure time was at ten at night and it got there at about ten the next morning. Only there was a big time change and it was actually 5 o'clock in Rome! Drew had already gotten his bag and had just gone off to grab a cart so they could haul their bags to the train area. Kate had purposely chosen a bright pink color bag, even though she intensely disliked the color, so that it would stick out on the belt in the sea of other black, brown, and burgundy bags. But she had seen at least 3 other bags the same color as hers. She was tired, hungry, and she was getting crabby. Drew was always patient and that was annoying her as well. Drew nudged her from behind and said "Hey I found a cart! Did your bag show up yet?" He said with his perfect smile and handsome face. Kate took a deep breath trying to not be crabby but geez she wanted to wipe that smug smile off his face! "Does it LOOK like I have my bag?" she said with her eyebrows raised, her head tilting towards the now empty baggage claim belt for their flight. Drew leaned over her and saw that no more bags were on the belt. "Um, ok, sorry, honey, let's go find out what happened to your bag. They walked over to the counter and were told that her bag was lost. They would track it and send it to their hotel as soon as they found it. Drew gave the address to the hotel and soon they were off, but all Kate could think about was that she was wearing underwear from the day before and she had not thought to stick some in her purse. She had however remembered a toothbrush. Drew still had to take his bag through customs and the line took about 15 minutes to get through. This was not helping Kate's crabby mood in any way, but she was trying not to be a poop. Seeing the crabby look on her face, Drew brought her in for a hug and told her everything would be alright and that "This stuff happens all the time," and not to worry. Drew led her outside to the train that would take about 35 minutes to get to Termini Station and then they would grab a cab for the short ride to the Hotel Fontana. Kate leaned against Drew as they sped down the countryside of Italy while she gazed out the window, worried about her undies.

It was nearly 6 o'clock by the time they got to Termini Station but there were plenty of cabs and they were at the hotel in 15 minutes. Kate got out of the cab and didn't even notice the hotel at all. It was directly in front of the Trevi Fountain. It was getting dark and the lights from the fountain lit up everything. Kate stood facing the fountain and walked slowly closer. There were quite a few tourists there but she made her way to the fountain. The water was an impossible clear blue as it cascaded down the middle. In the center, there were two marble horses on each side with men beside them, leading them possibly…Kate felt Drew's arm tugging at her elbow and she turned around. Her mouth opened; eyes wide………. *this* was the most beautiful thing she had ever seen! She was going to have to read up on the things they were going to see. Drew exclaimed, "Wow, this is so much prettier than it was in the brochure! Can you believe someone carved all the marble? You can see every muscle in the people and the horses!! But honey, let's get to our room and get settled and then we can come back and see this and get some dinner, ok?"

"Uh, yes, sorry Drew, I just couldn't help myself," she said. As they made their way through the crowd of people, Drew was saying "Scusami, scusami, per favore," (Excuse me please).

"Certamente signore!" (Certainly sir!).

"Sei americano?" (Are you American?), a kind gentleman asked. Kate understood that and said "Yes! Do you speak English?" The man laughed and said "No, no only Coca-Cola, New Yorrrk e Cheecago beers. Buona notte! Buona notte! Americanos!" He waved them a good night.

Kate and Drew finally made it into the hotel and into their lovely room that faced the Trevi Fountain. Kate took in everything she could in her new surroundings. Everything was so different here! All the floors were marble; the rooms were very different from American hotels. Each bathroom had a bidet and Kate wasn't quite sure how to use it. It made no sense to her that you would hover over a low toilet shaped sink and wash your bum. Kate needed to wash her only pair of underwear and decided the bidet would be good for that. Hanging them up in the shower, Kate went over to the little terrace that was off the back of their room. The Trevi Fountain looked gorgeous as the sun set which caused the fountain to look ablaze. It was a sight to behold! Kate was anxiously waiting for Drew to put his things in the large armadio on the far wall of the room. The room itself was not very large but had everything they needed. The small tv was on an antique table. The hotel was old, the walls of the room were stucco, and the ceilings were beamed in a dark wood. Drew excused himself to go and wash up in the bathroom after their long travels. Kate was very hungry and she must admit - terrified she would not get her clothes by tomorrow. First thing she must get out to the shops and buy a few things to tide her over until her own could be located and brought to her. Kate checked herself in the mirror, grabbed her purse and brushed her hair and touched up her makeup with the few things she had in her purse. When Drew came out, he kissed her soundly, but Kate pushed him away saying she needed to brush her teeth. Kate hurried into the bathroom and got some warm water going in the sink. She was NOT going to use the bidet to clean down there. With her luck, the water would squirt everywhere and ruin the only clothes she had left. After a thorough clean up Kate felt refreshed and felt weird because she was going to be going out without underwear. She wasn't from the generation that either wore none or wore a thong. She didn't even see the point of that at all. Coming out of the bathroom, Drew wiggled his eyebrows up and down and said, "So going commando tonight huh?" Kate laughed and said "Yeah I am pretty wild tonight! Let's go eat -I'm starving!!" Drew took her in his arms and kissed her deeply and Kate felt the stirrings…. he could make her forget anything except the heat from his mouth. "Drew, if you feed me, then I will be refueled to start our first beautiful night in Italy Then, my love, we will come back to the hotel, and I will show you how much I love you!" Drew laughed his sexy laugh and they left.

They headed toward the Spanish Steps which were only a half mile from the hotel. Crowds of people were everywhere in the piazza (a piazza is a large open area where people gathered) near the fountain, they had to almost push their way through to go down the Strada (street). The cobblestone streets were narrow and were worn shiny by time and use. Apartments, on either side of the road, rose up. Kate looked up and could see small balconies with flowers draping down. It made the street look romantic in the early evening while the sun was setting, casting fiery orange, yellow, and reds on the building walls making them appear as a painting. It really looked like the pictures she had seen but now she was here!

Kate's arm was linked through Drews as they came upon a doorway to one of the buildings. There was no sign on the outside of the building but as they peered in, there was a tiny restaurant tucked inside. They ducked inside and looked around seeing carafes of red wine on every table, Kate counted 6 square tables. In the back of the tiny room, there was a huge pizza oven, a gentleman was using a long stick to stir the coals. Two others, that were younger, were tossing pizza dough in the air and singing, while the patrons, of all races, clapped along and laughed. Drew was lucky enough to get a table and they sat down. Drew poured her a glass of wine. These glasses looked more like small jam jars to Kate, but at this point she would have sucked the wine out of the tablecloth. Drew raised his glass to hers and they clinked glasses and he said, "Alla nostra prima notte in Italia, amore mio!" (To our first night in Italy my love!). He leaned in and gave her a kiss over the table. There was no menu, there was only pizza. One of the men tossing pizzas came over and said "Buona sera! Pizza, pizza!" He said laughing, his eyes full of joy. He pointed to pictures on the wall of the five kinds of pizza and they agreed on Pizza Margarita. While they waited, Kate looked around at this little hole in the wall filled with laughter of people at the other tables. There was an air of romance everywhere within the soft lighting of the room and the glow off the fireplace that was cooking the pizza. It took no more than 5 minutes for their pizza to be ready. The man happily brought it over to the table on the wooded slab and slid it onto a flat stone. He cut it right there at the table and said "Mangiare felice!" (Happy eating!). The pizza looked so good and so different than any pizza she had had in the States. Kate and Drew both picked up a slice and took a bite. As was Kate's nature with food, she closed eyes and allowed all of the flavors on her tongue to unpack themselves. Her head rolled back as she took another and another bite. She was making *those* noises again and Drew nudged her and said, " Honey? Shhh, we are in public!" Kate opened her eyes and giggled at Drew. She lowered her voice and said "Sorry! You know how I am….I couldn't stop myself if I was in the front pew at church! Is this not the best pizza you have ever had in your life?!"

"Remember I was telling you about my friend who had been to Rome? He was the one who told me about this little out of the way place and that it was **literally** a hole in the wall with no sign." Drew said, wiping the sauce off his mouth with his paper napkin. Kate brought her napkin up as well and wiped the sauce from her own lips. Kate loved how happy the guys running this little place were. The atmosphere felt like you were at their house, and it was really heartwarming.

After they ate and finished the carafe of wine, they strolled down the narrow road noticing that cars were not using it. Lots of people were out in pairs and groups walking around this magical city in the evening; it was truly enchanted. Music seemed to be everywhere! Drew and Kate passed by a Trattoria. These little places were everywhere, with seating outside and served simple Italian food. They decided to try one of these places tomorrow. On the walk back to their hotel, they encountered a little place that was lit up called a Gelateria. They peeked inside and saw a narrow shop with an open cooler that held many rows of homemade Italian ice cream. Drew led the way into the shop, and they scanned the beautiful rows of gelato. It was going to be hard to pick just one! But Kate chose a coffee flavor and Drew , who was bolder, chose a cream and sour cherry flavor. They walked out into a piazza and sat on the edge of a fountain. Kate was noticing that when you walked to the end of a road, you came to a circle, like a roundabout, but in the middle were water fountains. This one had four maidens that held water pitchers with the water pouring out from them. It was so beautiful because they were all lit up. Drew put his arm around Kate and whispered in her ear. "Is this real? Are we really here doing this? It's our first night and I am so blown away by this experience!" Kate leaned back and looked in his eyes and he saw tears rolling down her face. "I never, in my wildest dreams, imagined I would come here, Drew. Our lives have had some tough stuff in it, and I just feel so blessed to be here with you right now!" If she had not turned her head back, she would have noticed that Drew had tears spilling down his own face. Finishing their yummy treat, they found a nearby trash. Their body clocks were going through some changes as it was heading toward 9pm in Italy - but they were not feeling ready for sleep. They strolled back to the hotel, arm in arm and enjoyed the sights and sounds of the evening in Rome.

When they got back to the hotel, the man at the front desk waved them over and said Kate's bag had been found and put in their room. Kate was overjoyed that she would not have to waste time or money on new clothes. They went to the room and she unpacked her things, setting aside a sexy nightgown for tonight.

Later that night, Kate could hear Drew's soft snoring and she smiled softly to herself. He was a wonderful, passionate lover and she never dreamed how much fun they would be having together. Kate quietly pushed back the blanket, not wanting to wake him, as she stepped over to the small balcony that overlooked Trevi Fountain. For about the tenth time tonight, she pinched herself to make sure she wasn't dreaming. It was about 3 am and there were still a few people out by the fountain. Young lovers, Kate imagined. While gazing out the window, Kate could not help but think of where her life had gone in the last two years. Change was hard for anyone and she was no stranger to it. She was thinking about how at now 53, she never expected her life to go this way. From the quiet, too busy, introverted author and now where she was with Drew! Their relationship had blossomed like a flower in full bloom. Now that they were getting to know one another better, the outside petals fell off to expose their deepest thoughts, fears, imperfections, quirks, and annoying habits but also the depth of their faith, their passion for their children, their families, and hobbies. Kate felt so inspired and thankful. She needed her life to mean something. She wanted to leave behind some sort of legacy and not just be known for being the poor young widow. Her and Drew had talked in depth about what this trip would be like. They both had things that were on the must-do list and it was not the same for both of them. They had to compromise on a few things but in the end, they were going to have a lovely trip. While Kate had wanted to jump on the tour buses and see all the sites of Rome, Drew hated the thought of being stuffed on an overcrowded bus and didn't care to see every church in the city. That, in itself, would take weeks or even months. So, they agreed to go to the ones that meant the most to Kate. They would use cabs and Ubers except when they went to see the Catacombs, they needed a tour bus for that but that was on Drew's must-do list and it was only **one** bus. Tomorrow, they would go to the Vatican, see the Sistine Chapel, and the Colosseum. They made no plans for where to eat because they wanted to wing that part of it. Let the place choose them! Kate turned back to see Drew turn over, feel that her side was empty, and leaned up on his elbow then patted the empty space. She slipped in between the blankets and Drew pulled her against him.

Chapter 2

Back at home, Addie nervously sat in the principal's office feeling as afraid as she had as a child. Having been summoned at the end of the day yesterday, she worried and wondered what this was about. She had been back at the private school for two weeks now and things, she thought, had been going really well. She met with first and second grade students several times a day in small groups to help them through their learning challenges. Addie not only loved her job but she also loved these children and couldn't imagine doing any other job. For her it was a calling. She felt a rumbling in her stomach and rubbed her hand over her belly. It was only slightly bigger from the pregnancy. She was grateful that the 12 weeks had passed, she wasn't as tired as she had been and could now keep food down again. But the nerves of waiting was making her pukey. Just then, Addie heard the squeak of the door as it opened and Mr. Kaplan called her into his office He shut the door behind her and motioned her to sit in the chair opposite his desk. Mr. Kaplan had thick, dark eyebrows and large thick black framed glasses. Those eyebrows were pressed together tightly making Addie think of a fuzzy caterpillar. "Ahem, Ms. Asher," he said nervously clearing his throat. "It has been brought to my attention by a few parents that you are pregnant?"

Addie nodded her head in the affirmative, "Why yes I am! Is that a problem?"

"Not at all under other circumstances, and you certainly are not breaking any laws, however, we do have a morale clause in your contract. Because this is a private school, some of the parents are concerned that because you are not married, that perhaps your decision-making skills are not a portrait of a good example to set for the young children you help." Addie's eyes grew large. She had not thought about it being a problem, women had babies all the time on their own without being married. In this day and age, who cared anymore? She rubbed her forehead and asked, "Am I being fired?"

"If you are getting married soon, we would be able to keep you on. However, if you choose to do this on your own, I'm afraid that because of the morale clause in your contract, we will have to let you go. I'm so sorry and this is not my call but it's coming down from the school board." Speechless, and near tears, Addie stood up on shaky legs and left the office. She went back to her small office near the front of the school, ran in quickly and closed the door making it to her desk before breaking down in tears. She had signed that contract but it had never occurred to her that she would be in the situation she was in, pregnant and not married. Addie and Joe had plans for the future but wanted the baby born before getting married. Now, she felt like she had to choose between her job and her baby. She texted Joe to meet her after work at her place. Joe was an IT man

13

for a well-established company. He texted back asking if she was ok and she responded with "DRAMA AT WORK." She wished her mom was here to talk things over with. She wished she was closer with her grandmother, although cordial, they still were not close. She wished her roommate was home but she had gone out of town on business and wouldn't be back for a few days. Jan popped into her head and Addie called her and asked if she could stop by in an hour but Jan was at the grocery store working and said she could stop by after work. Frustrated that everyone was busy right now, Addie looked at the clock, she had another group of kids to teach in ten minutes after which she would be done for the day. Pushing herself up, she rubbed her hands over her tummy and said, "Don't worry little one, we will figure this out." Since it was Friday Addie suggested that she and Joe go to Cedarcrest Lake and stay at her mom's for the weekend. He loved the idea. She went back to her place to pack for the weekend. Joe would pick her up after he stopped at home for his things.

The traffic heading north was awful! Even though it was only an hour away, it seemed to take forever in the stop and go traffic. Duh! Everyone wanted to go north on the weekend! Addie was crabby. She wanted to get to her mom's house before sharing her news with Joe. It was going to be an uncomfortable conversation and a peaceful setting might help them stay calm. Finally. getting to the cabin an hour and a half later, Joe grabbed their bags and brought them in the house. Addie noticed that Neal's truck was parked at Jan's house. She had hoped to talk to Jan about her situation, but she seemed to be busy tonight. Addie brought groceries and got to work on dinner for them. While not as good of a cook as her mom, she could hold her own in the kitchen. Joe, like his dad, was good on the grill so Addie handed him the chicken to be cooked on the grill. She cut up multicolored mini potatoes, mixed them up with some fresh herbs and olive oil, and got them roasting in the oven. She made a simple salad with romaine lettuce, tomatoes, green olives (which she was obsessed with ever since she found out she was pregnant!), and some Parmesan cheese. Joe liked *everything* and was not picky.. "Honey? How long on the chicken? I want to run to the bakery and get something sweet for dessert," Addie asked as he was coming in the kitchen to grab a beer out of the fridge. "Uh, it's going to be about a half hour, so you have time." He said, coming over to give her a hug. "Hey honey, I am the happiest man alive! I'm so glad we got to get away from the Cities - where it's just us and the quiet. I love you so much, and I cannot wait to meet our child." Addie's heart melted into a puddle. How did she get so lucky to find such a kind man? So many guys now were just into making money and sleeping around as much as they could. They were not into commitment. Joe was a serious person but knew how to have fun, too. Addie knew when she and Joe talked out her problem with the school, that he would be sensible unlike her with her raging pregnancy hormones. "I am so lucky, Joe. I love you so much too! I'll be back in 20 minutes, okay? This baby is needing something with chocolate!" She said giving him a kiss goodbye. She grabbed the keys off the counter and ran out to the car.

"Yoo HOO!" Jan called out. "Hello dear! Neal and I are going to have some dinner, did you two want to come over afterward and we can talk and sort things out?" Jan was so thrilled to be close to Addie. She had not been able to have children. Kate had become like a daughter to her and now Addie, a granddaughter. "Hi Jan!! Joe and I are going to eat dinner too. I'm just running to the bakery quick to get a treat for us for dessert."

"Oh honey! The bakery is closed. It closes at 6. But I was there today and got some chocolate filled croissants - I have plenty! You guys come on over whenever tonight, okay? If you get too tired, we can talk tomorrow too, whatever you need sweet pea." Addie walked over to Jan and hugged her.

"Thanks Jan, I think that is exactly what I was craving! You must have Grandma superpowers!" Addie could smell a lovely, soft perfumy scent coming off of Jan and it made her miss her mom- even though she had only been gone for a few days. It's just that she was *so* far away.

Addie went back in the house and joined Joe out on the deck. Joe was watching the people on the lake doing the evening boat parade. It was a spectacular evening. The sun was setting earlier now and the leaves were starting to change. Summer was nearing the end, and as most Northerners do, they start to panic a little when they see the leaves begin to change. It meant winter was not far behind. Addie went up behind his chair and circled her arms around him. He pulled her around on his lap and snuggled into her neck. She decided that to put off the conversation any longer was just going to stress her out. Standing up and walking across the patio she sat in a seat opposite him. "So Principal Kaplan called me into his office yesterday. Apparently, when I signed my contract I failed to notice there is a 'morale clause' in there. He said that some parents had heard I was pregnant and that, as an unwed mother, they would prefer I not teach their children. Something about my" lack of ability in the decision-making process". Because I got pregnant. I have a decision to make. Either I quit my job or we have to get married much sooner then we planned." Her eyebrows were pressed together and she rubbed her forehead. Joe stared at her but had no expression on his face. Addie gave him time to take in what she said. After a few minutes, he stood up, and walked over to her. She was sitting on the wicker loveseat. She looked up at him and saw the love in his eyes. Kneeling down, Joe said, "Addie, love of my life, will you marry me sooner than we planned?" He laid his head in her lap and rubbed her tummy.

"Joe! I never wanted you to have to be forced into marrying me because we got pregnant! I don't want it to be because I might lose my job!" Addie said as she raised up his head to look at her. Joe joined her on the loveseat. "Addie, we have been a little bit stupid. **WE** got pregnant. But that doesn't change the fact that we were going to get married anyway. This speeds it up a little. How could you ever stop teaching those kids? You love them! They love you! You are so gifted at what you do! You're so special! So, what if we speed things up a little. How about this -we go to the courthouse, get legally married and then after the baby is born, we can have a wedding? That way, you keep your job, and we get the wedding we both want!" Addie stood up and walked over to the grill checking on the chicken, killing some time while she thought. "How could I get married without my mom?" She wondered. "I won't be able to wait for a month while she is gone, should we keep it a secret or tell everyone?" She shared her thoughts with Joe. "Let's call your mom and tell her what we are going to do. We will just say simple vows and then when your mom gets back she can help us plan our real wedding. I'm sure she would not want you to lose your job over this. Dad has international texting on his phone, so I'll text him to set up a time for the four of us to talk that works for everyone. How does that sound?" Addie walked over to Joe and put her arms around his waist pulling him into her. He held her tightly and rubbed his hands through her long blond hair. "Oh Joe, you're the most amazing guy! I adore you! So, we're doing this?" She said looking up into his beautiful blue eyes. He kissed sweetly and said, "I can't wait for you to be Mrs. Johnson!!" Having made the decision, he pulled the chicken from the grill, they ate dinner and discussed plans for the courthouse wedding. They would need a license and some witnesses. Addie told him they were invited next door for dessert and they decided to ask Jan and Neal to stand up with them. Neal was Joe's grandfather, if his dad couldn't be there the next best thing was his grandfather whom he dearly loved. They walked hand in hand over to Jan's house next door..

Addie and Joe knocked on the door, but Jan leaned out from her deck facing the lake and said,   " Come through here, we are out on the deck!" They made their way through her year-round cabin to the back of the house and greeted the older couple that were enjoying a glass of wine. Jan jumped up and brought out a plate with the chocolate croissants. Addie's eyes lit up like a Christmas tree as she took one the of delicious treats with a napkin and sat down. Joe passed on the sweet concoction but took the beer offered by his grandpa. "How are you kids? So great having you up here for the weekend! How are things going Addie? Are you feeling better yet?" Neal said having grabbed a few blankets for the girls. It was cooling off a bit and he thoughtfully covered the ladies with some warm soft blankies. "Thanks Neal, that was sweet of you! Well, we have some news to share and would like some input from you," Addie said sweetly, sipping on the tea Jan had offered her. Jan's eyes got a little big but she understood that these two kids were known for dropping bombshell news. She took a deep breath and waited for the news to be shared.

Neal spoke first, after hearing about what had happened at Addie's job and their plans to do a quicky wedding. " I think you kids are doing the right thing. You planned on getting married, so this is good news! Have the wedding you want after the baby and continue to bless those kids with your God given gift. No one is perfect and because it's a private school they do have a leg to stand on. Jan? What are your thoughts?" He said taking her hand and rubbing his thumb over the back of it.

"I agree with Neal, you signed the contract with the morale clause, so I understand where they are coming from. I think you are taking responsibility by getting married and being able to keep your job to continue to be a blessing for those children. If you weren't planning on marrying anyway it would be a whole other situation. Well!! Congratulations!! It looks like there will be two weddings this year! Neal and I are going to have a small private ceremony at his house. Just close friends and family. I am delighted to part of your family!"

"Oh, Jan we are so happy to have you!!" With that the couples parted ways. Addie was exhausted after the long day and couldn't wait to go to sleep even though it was only 9:30. Growing a person was quite tiring, she thought as she rested her head on the fluffy pillow. She sighed as Joe pulled up the down quilt and covered his lovely bride to be. He was so excited about her becoming his wife and the mother of his child.

Chapter 3

"What do you mean Addie is pregnant? She's not married! What is going on in this family?! Does being loose run in our blood?" Kate's mother, Evelyn, shook her head in disgust.

"Now Evelyn, I thought we had come to a place of forgiveness and healing. Times are different now and Addie did say they *are* getting married. Please don't start up again, otherwise we will not be included in family functions. I am just NOW getting to know our grandchildren and now we have a great grandchild on the way! I will not have it this time!!" Peter said angrily at his wife. He stomped off and went out to the garden in the back of the house to blow off some steam.

"Well! I never!" Evelyn said to the back of his head as he slammed the door on the way out. How dare he speak to her that way! She prided herself on being able to keep him under her thumb all of their 55 years of marriage. He was the only boyfriend she had ever had and she was his only girlfriend. From a small town, they were basically the only two kids left standing without mates, so they got married. It was not a marriage of love but of convenience. They had grown to tolerate one another over the years. Evelyn had produced one offspring and that was that! They had become upstanding in the community and in their church. Evelyn was a big fish in a small pond there. Being on the board of the church, gave her an air of superiority and she liked it that way. Over the last two years, though, she had been talked into attending one of the church's small groups that met on Wednesday mornings that was called the Silver Foxes. Evelyn had, for once in her life, been vulnerable with these woman about her daughter getting pregnant as a teen and forcing her to give the child up for adoption. A few months after that, she'd had a stroke and in her weakened state, Evelyn had finally apologized to her daughter. She had met the young man called Jake who was her oldest grandson and thought him a fine young man. She honestly had no regret about what she had done but told her daughter otherwise so they could have a relationship. It was still strained but at least it was something. Her heart had grown cold to love years ago when she was a child. An only child herself, her parents seemed to resent her mere presence, they and were often cold and unfeeling towards her. They took care of all her physical needs, but she had always been lacking for love. This had made Evelyn bitter and she took it out on as many people as she could. How dare THEY get loved and not her. Her husband had tolerated her for all these years. Peter needed someone to take care of him and she did her duty as a wife. But there was very little love and almost no intimacy . She had closed that part of herself off after she gave birth to Kate, despite rumors about her husband finding love elsewhere. She really didn't care as long as they remained married. She had never asked him about it and he had never spoken about it.

Now, she looked out at him and shook her head. How was she going to explain this latest mess to her church friends?! Maybe she would wait until *after* the baby was born when they had been married for a while. Addie wouldn't be the first woman to have an 'early baby' within the first year of marriage. With the decision made, Evelyn went in to start dinner ignoring the ramblings of her husband out in the garden.

When her husband came in later, he walked right up to her as she set the table and said "Evelyn, you have been a cruel woman for the whole of our marriage and because I let you control me, we lost out on having relationships with our daughter and our grandchildren. I have asked myself over and over again why I stay, and right now that answer doesn't matter anymore. I am moving out and you should expect divorce papers from my attorney. I am done with your poison! I aim to be as close to our daughter and those grandchildren as I can for the rest of my life and YOU?? Well, YOU can sit in this house ALONE for the rest of yours and sit on your pious throne!" With that, he stomped upstairs. The thumps and bumps of drawers being pulled opened and closed resonated throughout the house. Evelyn, in shock, slowly sat down in the chair at the kitchen table. Her day of reckoning had come.

Hours later, she still sat in her chair of righteousness. It was dark out now and the house was quiet. The phone didn't ring because she had no true friends and her husband was long gone. Finally, the tears came as she finally let some feeling come to the surface. Maybe it was time to be honest with herself, everything truly was her fault. The dark thoughts came, her long forgotten secret brought to the surface, this was payback she thought. It was going to be a long, long night.

Chapter 4

Kate woke up to her neck being kissed, she turned, yawned, and stretched. Her first morning waking up in Italy!! She was self-conscious about her breath because, no matter how much she brushed she could still smell garlic on her breath. She cupped her hand over her mouth and blew in her hand several times testing her breath. Drew laughed at her saying, "Honey, I think it might be my breath you are smelling, sorry! I wonder if this might be our lot as long as we are here. I say if it is - it's a good one! Have you ever had better pizza in your life? And the Gelato was amazing! How can we ever go back to eating regular ice cream!?" Kate laughed, rubbed his beautiful salt and pepper chest hair, and got out of bed. She was not used to chatting much in the morning as it took her a bit longer to wake up than Drew. He knew this about her, and he jumped out of bed to begin his morning routine. First, Kate got cleaned up in the bathroom, chose some jeans, a yellow t-shirt, and some comfortable shoes for the day. Her hair was a disaster, so she threw it up in a messy bun and touched up her make-up. Drew loved how fast she got ready. He was ready for the day as well and they left to go to breakfast at the hotel.

What a charming dining room! The ceilings were plaster and wood beams, and the sides were all windows that were open with no screens! Something she had noticed on every building. "I guess they don't have the bugs that we do," she thought to herself. On a long table covered with a white tablecloth, there were coffee and tea urns with a stunning array of breakfast pastries. They filled their plates with the delicate treats, got tea, coffee, and juice then took them over to a table overlooking the Trevi Fountain. Drew noticed Kate pinching herself and said "I have been doing that so many times too! Are we really here?" She laughed, "I know I can't believe it either!!"

Their plans for the day were aggressive. The first stop was the Vatican, then the Sistine chapel, the Colosseum and then have dinner near Piazza Navona, one of the largest and most famous Piazzas in Italy. Piazza Navona was a large rectangle that was big enough to hold three separate fountains and Drew and Kate could hardly wait to go! They reminisced about how lovely Jake and Jenna's wedding was and how happy he seemed now. Kate had loved the simple but elegant wedding in Jakes parents' backyard garden. Jenna's parents were delightful people and welcomed Jake like a son. He was going to be so happy, and that's all Drew and Kate cared about. "Well," Drew said standing and taking Kate's plate, "Shall we get moving? We have a big full day ahead of us." A man came running over, hotel staff by the looks of his white coat, and said "Signore, signore no, per favore lascialo lasciare che è il nostro lavoro!" He gently took the plates from Drew and backed away bowing. "I have no clue what he said but I'm thinking he didn't want me bussing my own table! Ha ha ha ha ha!" Kate took out her phone and tried to translate the few words she could pick out. "Yes, I think he wants to take care of us. Let's let him do his job! We will learn as we go in this beautiful country my love, the Italian people will teach us their ways! I can't wait!"

They hailed a cab from near the Spanish Steps, which was a sight to behold in itself. Beautiful, wide steps that lead up to a balcony with a church at the top. There were flowers up and down both sides of the steps. There were vendors on various steps peddling jewelry and art. Some were handmade and some of the art was really pretty. Drew pulled her away from the vendors, reminding her that they had a big day ahead and they could stop by tomorrow. Making their way to Vatican City, the sights and sounds of Rome were like no other place she had been. Not that she had really been anywhere but the state of Minnesota. It was loud and the public transportation buses were everywhere and people drove wherever they wanted it seemed. There were no neat lines on the road to mark which lane to stay in. People just piled in wherever they could fit. The cars were all small so that helped! Kate looked at Drew in admiration for not renting a car to drive in this huge city.

Drew and Kate people watched as they wove their way through the city. The cab driver dropped them near the Vatican, they got out and walked toward the walled city. Vendors lined both sides of the street selling anything religious including cross necklaces, chips of splintered wood supposedly taken from Jesus' cross, little statues of Mary, prayer beads, little Bibles, Holy oil sold in tiny bottles, and the list went on and on. Kate wasn't into this kind of thing so it was easy for her to walk by and not be tempted. Drew took her hand, and they made their way through the center of the city that was a big circle surrounded by walls. On top of the wall, there were giant statues of, what she thought were the 12 Apostles. They entered the church and, like many tourists, walked around making noises of awe. The mosaics, the stained-glass windows, and the gold alter with the dark pillars that seemed to touch Heaven. They touched the foot on the statue of St. Paul, rubbed smooth by the millions who had gone before them. They stopped at the statues called La Pieta. It was one of Michelangelo's finest. It depicted Mary, the mother of God, sitting and holding the body of the crucified Jesus in her arms. Kate stared for a long time and wept. She noticed others around her doing the same. Drew handed her a tissue and led her to the Sistine Chapel and was mesmerized by the angelic talent of Michelangelo's ceiling. There was almost too much to see in one visit but they were on a schedule and had to get on to the Colosseum.

The Colosseum was a massive oval amphitheater built and finished around 70 to 80 AD. It was used for entertainment and could hold around 80,000 spectators. As seen in movies, Kate and Drew talked about the Gladiator contests, animal hunts, and how they used to re-enact battle scenes. Later, it was used for housing, workshops, quarters for religious orders, and a Christian shrine. The mobs of people around them joined in their viewing and they could overhear conversations in English. Stray cats also seemed to be everywhere, while friendly for the most part, there were some really weird looking cats in the bunch. Turning away and heading out, Drew told her that the Colosseum had been substantially ruined by an earthquake. Kate was getting hungry and tired from all the walking she had done, and Drew said he was also ready for a break, his feet hurt too. At last!! Drew *is* human, Kate laughed to herself. Drew was not a complainer at all. She on the other hand was a bit of a baby when it came to physical suffering. It was getting late; they hailed a cab and told the driver they wished to go to Piazza Navona.

As they drove on the road next to the Tiber River, the ruins on either side of the road were lit up and it looked fake! Kate once again pinched herself to make sure she wasn't dreaming. The cab driver let them out and they walked into the large open area, four large fountains in the piazza were all lit up and there was a lovely gold glow on the buildings as the sun went down. It was magical. They chose a restaurant that had outside seating, which it seemed most did, at least this time of year. Ponte e Pacione, a charming place close to one of the fountains, looked so romantic and they were immediately seated by a young man in a crisp white shirt and small white towel over his shoulder. "Per favore, per favore, siderite e di porterò una lista di vini

Sir e Madame," He scurried off and quickly came back with a wine list and waited patiently for them to order. Drew looked up and said, "Do you speak English?"

"Sì, sì, certo. Yes, yes of course, how can I help you?" Kate thought his accent was very charming and he was not a bad looking man. "My name is Marco, and I am here to help you through this beautiful night." He scurried off and came back a short while later and poured their wine. "It sure is nice to sit down and relax! We had quite a day with all that we saw. I'm not going to sleep with all that rattling around in my head," Drew said taking in a deep breath and blowing it out. "Ah yes, it does feel so good to sit and have a glass of wine with my love, look around! Do you see all the young lovers gathering at the fountains? It is so romantic here!" Kate's eyes took on a dreamy state as she looked here and there. This wine was going right to her head! Whoa! Drew looked around as well, but he had food on his mind. The waiter came back and asked "Do you trust me? If so, I would like to show you why Italy has the best food and I would love to give you this experience, is this okay signor?" He asked looking at Drew. Kate thought this sounded amazing! Drew nodded his head, and the waiter came back with two bowls of steaming hot soup, it was a light broth with what looked like scrambled eggs and chives in it, it was delicious. Marco then took those away and brought them a dish that held lovely pillows of a squash ravioli in a brown butter sauce topped with zucchini flowers. It was the best thing Kate had ever tasted. This was why she was here, to eat amazing food. The wine was flowing and the ambiance like they had never experienced, as they enjoyed this incredible meal. Next, came lovely white fish in a white wine bechamel with rosemary roasted potatoes and caramelized rustic-colored carrots in a yummy, sweet sauce that Kate could not figure out. They ate slowly, they savored each bite and really tasted the flavors exploding in their mouths. Kate felt ready to burst and Drew leaned back sighing. A look of pure contentment on his face. The bottle of wine was empty, and Marco saw fit to bring a second. It had almost been two hours of eating! But it was slow and different than any experience she had ever had. It really was the celebration of the food *and* the people where they were, it was surreal. It was glorious. Marco then brought them a dessert she had never had. It was called zabaglione. Made with eggs yolks, sugar, and a sweet wine, it was almost like a custard but not, with freshly whipped cream on top and a pirouette cookie sticking out of the top. Kate was stuffed but sweets were her weakness. Drew rubbed his belly but dove in as well as the creaminess filled their senses. Kate thought she was going to have a seizure, her eyes rolled back in her head, and she started making her "Kate" noises. "Kate!! Uh, honey? You cannot make those noises in public! I know it's about the food, but others might think something funny is going on under the table!" He said laughing at her. That brought back the delightful memory of how they met, in the bakery while Kate was tasting her favorite almond

Danish. She had had her eyes closed then as well and was making very inappropriate noises! But she couldn't help herself! This was just her reaction to food that took her to another place. Like a traveler through the galaxies, only for her, it was a flavor journey. Marco finally brought out some Italian coffee and Drew realized it was well past 9. It had been a 12-hour day and he was ready to get back to their hotel. Giving Marco a generous tip and much gratitude for the exquisite dining experience, they walked through the piazza and out into the night and hailed a cab. It had been a wonderful first day.

∞∞∞∞∞∞∞∞∞∞∞∞∞∞∞∞∞∞∞∞

Addie paced back and forth in her living room while Joe sat on the couch waiting for the time to pass. His knees were nervously bouncing up and down. "Addie, we only have ten more minutes to wait before calling our folks! Try and relax, we are not giving them bad news or even shocking news so try to relax."

"Don't ever tell a woman to relax, Joe, it actually makes the opposite happen and makes me feel really crabby towards you!" Addie said giving him a dirty look. "Yikes!" Joe thought, those pregnancy hormones could come up and bite you right in the rear. He got up from the couch and walked to the kitchen and made her favorite cup of tea then brought it out to her. Kate had taught him that tea made everything better. He handed her the steaming, creamy, sugary cup of tea and she sighed then smiled. "Joe, you are so sweet to me! I get so crabby! I just want to get this over with and have her be happy for us and be okay that she won't be here!"

"Honey, it's going to all be okay. She will be so glad that you won't lose your job and we will have the big wedding and party after the baby is born." Joe rubbed her arm to reassure her.

Joe's phone stated buzzing as if listening to their conversation.

"Hey Dad! How is the trip going?"

"Hey Joe! Oh, we are having such a wonderful time! I'm sure glad I brought comfortable shoes although I will probably have to buy some new pants here with all the delicious food we are eating! How is Addie feeling? Oh, and just so you know you are on speaker phone and Kate is right here with me."

"Hi Joe and Addie, it's Mom! How are you feeling?"

"Hi Mom! I am feeling really good, just the typical fatigue that all pregnant moms feel. It's a lot of work growing a person!"

Drew, put his arm around Kate and brought her up next to him. "So, you guys wanted us to call. Of course, we are curious what that's all about."

"Well," Addie sighed, "We had a decision to make about my job. Apparently, I signed a morale clause and because I teach at a private school, some of the parents were concerned with the fact that I am unmarried and pregnant. The principal of the school said that if we don't get married soon then I will be fired. So, Joe and I are going to the courthouse next week and say our vows, but we still want to have a wedding and reception after the baby is born; just like we planned. Joe understands how much I love the kids and how much they love me and under other circumstances I might not make the same decision. I hope this won't be too hard on you, not to be here for that, but like I said, you will be here for the wedding. Mom, I just can't lose my job and I did sign that morale clause." Addie finally took a breath after talking really fast just to get the news out.

Kate's mouth hung open the whole time her daughter spoke. At first, she was really mad at the school, how dare they, this is not the dark ages! But after she heard about the morale clause, it really did make sense. "Addie, I agree with your decision, and while I will be sad that we aren't there when you say your vows, I can still be excited for your wedding. I love you honcy! I am so proud of you! You too, Joe, you guys are making the right decision."

"I second everything Kate just said. Joe, I'm proud of you as well. I would totally understand if you wanted to tell the school to shove it but it's not about that, it's about those kids and their relationship with you, Addie. That is the bigger issue. I think's it's great and shows real maturity to set aside your egos and do the right thing for the kids and for you too, Addie. You're going to make a wonderful mother." Drew said while holding Kate close, then kissing the top of her head.

"Thanks Dad, thanks Kate. We *are* really happy. Once we get married, I am having Addie move into my place until we can find a house. I have plenty of space at my condo for Addie and the baby. And it's better to move now before she gets too big."

"Joe has been great even through between the tears and the crabby outbursts. I have not been the nicest person to be around."

"Honey, everything will work out! Drew and I can help when we get back if you want to wait to move until then." Kate said as she watched out the window seeing the tourists jam in to see the Trevi Fountain. What a sight to see while you are chatting on the phone!

"I already have movers going to her place next week. I paid extra to have them pack up her things. Her roommate is bummed though. But she said her boyfriend is going to move in with her so everything will work out. He's a great guy, we have been doing some couple dates with them."

"I really like hearing how well my daughter is being cared for, Joe, sounds like you are a chip off the old block! Addie, you are one lucky woman if Joe is half the man Drew is!" said Kate.

"I have no complaints, Mom. So, we will call you next Friday after we say our vows. We will text you to let you know the time. Love you so much and thanks for your support and kind words. I know I'll still cry because my mama isn't there and I seem to have a gazillion tears in my body right now!"

"I love you too daughter! Cry a river if you want! I will be doing the same here."

"Okay kids, we are off to another adventure today. Love you both!! "Drew said and the call ended.

"I am really happy for those two. I think they are a good fit. Don't you?" Kate said applying some lipstick in the mirror.

"I do! Joe is a great guy and Addie is a sweet woman just like her mom. Now, let's head out to Borghese Park!! We have romantical things to do today!!"

"I know! This is on my bucket list! Let's go! Got your comfy shoes on? I am wearing a dress so I can eat more food. I know when I get back, I will be ten pounds heavier but I don't care right now. I want to eat my way through Italy! Will you join me, handsome man? "

"I feel like I have already gained weight, my jeans are getting snug. But we can do a lot of good walking at the park today. Tomorrow we are going to the Catacombs and we will get lots of good walking in then, too. So yes, my love!! Let's make some memories and eat our way through Italy!!" With that he walked over and put his arms around Kate, swung her around and passionately kissed her. He slowly set her down, she looked back at him and a fire had started him, and it got very warm in the room. The magic of Italy overtook them! Celebrare l'amore! They were going to be a little late getting to the park. And maybe burn a few calories.

Chapter 5

Evelyn walked through her house, room by room, and saw her husband's mark everywhere. A tie clip, his books on the nightstand, and his robe hanging on the back of the bathroom door. It had been over a week since she heard from him. Not even a phone call! She had lied to the women at church on Sunday and said that Pete was a little under the weather but assured them he was fine. He would be back. She had done *everything* for him and he would not be able to live without her cooking, cleaning, and washing his clothes. Just as she was coming down the stairs she heard a knock on the door. Ah! Finally, he has come crawling back to me! She thought as she made her way to the front door. Her upper lip stiffened, and she held her head high as she smugly opened the door. A man stood in front of her but it was not Pete.

"Evelyn Asher?"

"Yes, who wants to know?" He reached in his jacket and pulled out a manilla envelope and handed it to her saying, "You've been served," and quickly ran down the steps to his car and drove off. As he did, he looked at the stunned woman with her mouth hanging open, still standing in the doorway. He laughed to himself and thought, "That never gets old." She looked like a crabby old bat and probably had whatever was in that envelope coming to her. He drove off with his tunes cranked.

"I've been served? Served what?" Evelyn quickly shut the door but not before checking to her left and right to see if any neighbors had seen what just took place. Mr. Kelp from across the street stood at his mailbox staring at her. "Harrumph," she thought, "that old gossip!" She shut the door and walked quickly to the kitchen where she tore open the envelope and pulled out some thick papers. She gasped when she saw that it was a legal document from an attorney. It was for the dissolution of her marriage. Peter was divorcing her! She backed away and slowly sat down in her pink Queen Anne chair. She truly had not seen this coming. He said he was done with her but until this moment she thought he would come dragging his sorry butt back to her, full of apologies. She ran to the phone and tried to call him. He picked up on the second ring. "I guess this means you got the papers?" Peter said, he sounded different -strong and manly. "Uh yes, I just got them. I am shocked to say the least. You can't divorce me! Who will take care of you? You don't know how to take care of yourself!"

"I am 72 years old Evelyn, and you don't have to worry about me anymore. Whatever it takes to be free from your hateful poison then I will do it. I said I am done with you and I am."

"Well! I never!" Evelyn was so angry that she was shaking as she slammed the receiver of the house phone on the wall. How dare he! She was going to make his life a living Hell. She had heard of other nasty divorces and hers would be one as well.

Evelyn grabbed the paperwork and read through it. He was giving her the house and plenty of money. He was keeping her on his medical insurance, and she would get some money from his life insurance. He was letting her keep her car. There wasn't going to be much to fight about as he had been overly generous and fair. Well, at least she would have the house. She sat there for hours and began to wonder where it all went wrong. She had never *really* loved him. She thought he never *really* loved her either. She didn't believe in all that nonsense. That was for movies and books, not reality. Oh Lord, what would she tell the ladies from church? She would have to sell the house and move to where no one knew her. Yes, a clean slate. That's what she would do. She called a real estate agent and after a long talk, the house would go on the market as soon as the divorce was final. She didn't want to wait that long but she could not sell the house until it legally belonged to just her. She called Peter back and told him to get a court date as soon as possible. She wanted this sham over quickly. It had been a very draining day and she went up to lie down on her bed. Sometimes, life just seems to work out- for that night, while Evelyn slept, she had a massive stroke and died. There would be no divorce. Peter could move back into the house and the women of the church would never know. They would bring him food and be none the wiser. Evelyn, had she known, would be pleased. No one would know about the ugliness of the divorce, and no one would ever know about the secret she had kept for 54 years. She indeed would take it to her grave......only one other person knew, and she would never tell. Right?

∞∞∞∞∞∞∞∞∞∞∞∞∞∞∞∞∞∞∞∞∞∞∞∞∞∞∞∞∞∞∞∞∞∞∞∞∞∞

The small, short ceremony took place. Harry, and his girlfriend, Francesca, were there as witnesses as well as Neal and Jan. Addie had invited her grandfather, Peter, whom she had been connecting with over the last few weeks. Peter shared with them of the split from her grandmother and how he wanted to have a closer relationship with them. Addie was delighted! The more she got to know him, the more she could see what a kind man he was. She had not heard a word from her grandmother. Not surprising. She had not been pleased to hear of the baby, in her words "The shot gun wedding". Addie had given up a long time ago trying to please Evelyn or even trying to have any relationship with her. She thought for a while that the mini stroke she had might have caused some good changes in her; really, nothing had changed. So today, on her wedding day, (in her mind, her fake wedding day), Addie didn't mind that the negative woman wasn't here. Her grandfather explained that he had served her with divorce papers and, other than a phone call the same day, he had not heard from her either. No one cared. She had "made her bed", so to speak. Addie and Joe were glad Neal and Jan were there. They were happy, positive people and if she couldn't have her mom there with her, Jan was the next best thing. And Neal? Addie always thought Joe looked just like him and seemed to embody his kind spirit as well. There was a good vibe going on today.

Joe looked into Addie's eyes and spoke the simple vows in front of the judge. It was sweet, to see as an outside observer, how much in love these young people were and it warmed Peter's heart to see what love looked like. He hadn't had that. But maybe for him, now that he would be set free from bitterness, and a heart that had grown ice cold years ago, he might have a chance to love. He was so excited to be a part of his grandchildren's lives. He felt honored to be here today with Kate and Drew being in Italy and all. It was lovely and he offered to take everyone out for a nice dinner, which they gladly accepted.

Kate and Drew had been informed that the wedding had taken place and also that Peter had filed for divorce. Kate and Drew had heard the news in the phone call promised after the ceremony. Kate wasn't going to let anything spoil her time with Drew and would deal with that when they got home. She and Drew gave warm congratulations to the newly married couple and got back to enjoying what felt like a honeymoon.

∞∞∞∞∞∞∞∞∞∞∞∞∞∞∞∞∞∞∞∞∞∞∞∞∞∞∞∞∞∞∞∞∞

Kate and Drew rented bicycles when they got to Borghese Park and rode around the beautiful, landscaped gardens. There were several museums to see, and they spent a few hours going through them looking at paintings and sculptures. Afterward, they headed over to rent a small boat to ride around on the small lake there. While they were in line for tickets, they met a group of Americans. It was a group of eight guys that looked to be about their age. They said they were in a band and were playing at a nightclub near Trevi Fountain. They invited Kate and Drew to be their guests that night. It was fun to meet some fellow Americans- and, these guys were from Wisconsin! Kate loved country music as did the Italians. It sounded really fun. Drew, while not as much of a country fan, was happy to meet up later with these guys. They were really nice! It was fun to meet people from the same neck of the woods they were from.

Kate sat in the back of the boat while Drew rowed. Kate laughed and said she felt like she was in a movie, the only thing missing was an umbrella to cover her face. She did have a cute dress on though and Drew kept telling her to lean back. "Lean back honey, when you do, I can see up your dress! Ha ha ha!"

44

"Drew Johnson! You dirty old man!! "

"I'm sorry, my love, x but you make it difficult to be a gentleman sometimes."

The night club, the band was playing at, was called the M1 . You had to walk down into a cave-like atmosphere. It was really neat how they worked the lighting and the club was quite large. Kate and Drew chose a spot closer to the front to see the band better. The guys from the band waved at them and they waved back. It was a fun night of dancing! Drew was a good sport even though country music was not his favorite. During a break, some of the guys from the band came over and visited with Kate and Drew. The drummer was talking with Kate, he said his name was Thomas. They talked about living in Minnesota and Wisconsin and how much they loved it. Drew was staring at them, came over and said, "I never noticed this until you two were standing next to each other, but you look like you could be twins! Wow! Kate, did you notice?" It was not well lit in the bar so she really had not gotten a good look at him. They now looked at each other from head to toe as Tom laughed as he told them his break was over and they would talk more later.

Kate was a little shook up as she watched Tom walk back behind his drum set and begin to play. She sat slowly back down, and Drew kept staring at him. "This guy literally looks just like the male version of you! I guess you've met your doppelganger." He blew if off as nothing, but Kate couldn't take her eyes off him. She felt really strange. Like the thing that was missing in her was no longer missing. She couldn't put her finger on this feeling. It wasn't like a huge chasm, but it was like she found the last piece of the 1000-piece puzzle. "Hmmm," she thought.

Chapter 6

After her examination, the doctor confirmed, not only the pregnancy, but that she was to have twins. Evelyn could not believe her rotten luck. Not only did she get pregnant the first time she and her new husband consummated the marriage at his insistence, but now she was pregnant with twins! She hadn't wanted children at all. Her own parents showed her how much of an annoyance they were and treated her like a pesky gnat. Caring for her basic needs but not caring much about her at all, Evelyn was an only child that had often gotten dropped off at a cousin's in Wisconsin while her parents traveled. She had grown up with her cousin, Marsha, and they were both awkward, ugly. and shy.. Had it not been for each other, neither of them would have had any friends. They played like little girls do in the country with very little money and found things to do outside - where they were constantly being shooed to go. "Go out and play!" Her grumpy uncle, Leo, would say. He was Marsha's father, who was crabby <u>all</u> the time. He always smelled of beer and cigarettes, which was understandable, since he also had a filter less smoke hanging off his lip. Like many farmers, he worked from sunup to sundown so there was very little joy in the house. Evelyn's parents paid them a small fee for keeping her when they were gone, which was a lot to Leo.

As Evelyn sat in the old doctor's office, she thought of her cousin, Marsha. Marsha wanted kids and had been unable to have any. She had told Evelyn about the several miscarriages she had endured. Evelyn began to formulate a plan even before she got to her car.

When Evelyn got home, she called Marsha. She told her she had a plan and they needed to meet to discuss it. Marsha was intrigued. They agreed to meet halfway where no one knew them. Peter was at work all day so he wouldn't know she would be gone. He carpooled with a guy that lived down the street so Evelyn had the car to run her errands every day. Agreeing to meet tomorrow, Evelyn worked out the plan in her head and she hoped that Marsha was desperate enough to go along with it.

The next day, they met in a tiny town that only had a church, gas station and a café. Marsha was already there waiting for her, and Evelyn made her way over to the back table of the grimy café. This place needed a good cleaning, thought Evelyn, but she had bigger things on her mind.

"So, Cousin, what it the big plan? What is the big secret?" Marsha asked.

"I am pregnant with twins; I can barely stand the thought of having *one* let alone *two*. I want you to have one of the babies. We need to find a doctor who will deliver the babies, and then give one to you. A doctor, perhaps, that is in debt and we can pay him off. Do you know anyone like that?"

"Hold on! You are going to give me one of your babies? How can you do that?"

"You know I didn't want kids, and here I am stuck with two in my belly. Peter knows I'm pregnant, but I am not going to tell him it's twins. You get one and I get one. We just need to figure out the details."

"Well, I know of a doc that is one town over- who is a drunk and always broke, would you feel safe having him deliver you? He has the women come right to his clinic to have the kids there. I guess I have never heard of anything bad happening as far as that goes," Said Marsha.

"I've had some time to think about this, so, when I am getting close to my due date - I will tell Peter that I am coming for a visit. You pretend you are pregnant. Hopefully you can tell Bud our plan so he goes along with it. I know how desperate he is for a son. Then, when I go into labor, I will have the babies at this doc's office - if we can pay off his silence. I have $5000.00 saved for 'just in case' money. Do you have any? I would hope he would do it as this is a large sum of money for a country doctor. He needs to be onboard with this plan or the deal is off. No adoption, just we both walk in pregnant, and we both walk out with a baby."

"Wow! You sure have put a lot of thought into this plan. Are you sure about this? If I bring that baby home, I don't want you changing your mind and taking it back. You know how long I have been wanting a baby."

"Marsha, I don't want *any* babies at all, but Peter knows I'm pregnant and unless I miscarry, I'm stuck."

"Okay, well, the first thing for me to do is tell Bud to see if he will agree to this plan. Knowing how badly he wants a child; I am thinking he will be excited.. The next thing is to let Bud, and I check into this doctor over in Orm, and see if we can bribe him to go along with our plan." Marsha looked around the greasy café and was glad to see no one paying them any attention. It was mostly old, widowed farmers who couldn't make their own breakfast that were stuffing their faces with runny egg yolk sticking to their mouths. "Let's talk again this week but we have to be careful what we say on the phone. Why don't you tell Peter that you are going to come for a visit, and I should have some answers for you by then."

"Sounds good, but we have to have this plan in place soon. I am due in five months. I know sometimes twins come early, so I would have to stay with you a month before I am due. Peter is almost as naïve as I am when it come to this baby stuff." Both women had finished their coffee and toast. They stood and the old wooden chairs made a loud sound. People turned to stare at them with slow eyes and a great lack of concern. They didn't care at all. Good. Marsha and Evelyn headed to their respective cars excited but for each woman a different reason.

It had been so easy to fool Peter as they didn't sleep in the same bed and there was very little affection between the two of them. It had been a marriage of convenience for both of them. Evelyn would be kind to him, take care of him, but she was not interested in the intimate part of marriage. She knew, though, that she had to do her duty but had been given a pass while she was pregnant. She pretended to be as excited about the baby as Peter. He had given her money to fix up a nursery which she had done. They had just started going to a new church after they got married and had moved to St. Paul for his job. The gals at church had thrown her a shower and had commented on how big she was. She laughed to herself knowing why. She did try to control her weight as much as possible, eating only enough food so that she didn't feel hungry. Peter had no clue. Evelyn had met Marsha and Bud a few weeks after the cousin's initial meeting and the plan was in place. The doctor was more than happy to be onboard with a plan where no one got hurt and he could make some fast cash . In his mind, he was doing a good thing for a woman who could not bear a child herself.

A month before the baby was due, Evelyn told Peter she was feeling restless. She told him she wanted to go and visit Marsha for a week and reassured him she would be fine. It was only an hour's drive and they had a hospital in town if anything happened. Peter was very anxious but she would **not** take no for an answer. In her suitcase, she packed some tiny clothing to bring of which to bring her baby home. When she got to Marsha's house, Bud was so excited and treated Evelyn like a princess. She was not to lift a finger. They also had a nursery set up. Marsha had stuffed a round pillow up her shirt and, indeed, looked to be almost nine months pregnant. Marsha and Bud told all of their friends as Martha mimicked the symptoms of a pregnancy as Evelyn told her about them. So far, so good! The cousins had a nice time together, sitting outside in the evenings and Bud would bring them desserts and coffee out on the back porch.

Evelyn went to bed one evening and rubbed her sore back. She would be glad to have this over with. She didn't enjoy pregnancy at all. She fell into a fitful sleep and was awakened by sharp pains in her belly. She sat up in bed and was happy! She thought-, "This was it and it's only been four days! I was right! The twins are here early! She slowly got up from the bed and made her way to her cousin's bedroom and woke them both up saying "It's time!" Bud jumped out of bed and ran around like a chicken with its head cut off. "BUD!!!!" yelled Marsha. "Get your act together! Grab the bag we packed and then get Evelyn's' bag. I will help Evelyn to the car. Now GO!!" Bud snapped out of it and threw his clothes on while the ladies made their way to the car. He got there at the same time. "I forgot to call Doc to tell him we were coming! I'll be right back." Bud ran back into the house which was fine with Evelyn as she held onto the car door as a strong contraction gripped her. "Wow - this hurts a LOT!" Beads of sweat broke out on her forehead and the September air did nothing to help cool her brow. Bud came running back out saying the doc was heading over to the clinic.

It was like the plan was meant to be; everything went perfectly. The labor part, of course, was not fun but two healthy children were born. A boy and a girl. Evelyn felt nothing inside as the doctor handed a beautiful dark-haired baby boy over to her cousin. Bud had tears rolling down his face as he held his son for the first time. Evelyn had done well, with no complications, and the doctor was paid his fee for his silence. He was going to be able to pay off some gambling debts and that was good. After helping Evelyn into the back of the car with instructions of what dangers to watch out for, the new families sped off in the wee hours of the morning. It was a dark, stormy morning and Bud barely got the women and babies into the house before the angry skies broke open and the thunderstorm raged for several hours. Evelyn rested in the guest room with her new baby, she decided to call her Kathryn. She would call Peter later after she slept. Marsha was wonderful, taking care of her and fed Kathryn along with her new son, Thomas. Evelyn would not nurse. It sounded disgusting to her.

"What? You had the baby? Are you alright? Is the baby alright? What is it?" Peter drilled her with questions like rapid gunfire. She gave him the good news that everything was fine and that they had a daughter that she named Kathryn. In a few days, Bud would drive her home. Peter went crazy having to wait but there was no way she could have let Peter come there and see another baby. The secret started NOW. He finally agreed and she gave him a list of things to get at the store in preparation of their arrival. He was happy to have something to do and grateful to his neighbor for letting him use his car. Peter had told the whole neighborhood about the new baby. The gals from church had come and dropped off some meals for the new family. Peter had paid for a woman to come in and give the home a fresh clean. He was so excited! Today, he was going to meet his baby girl. He looked down the road in anticipation of their arrival. Soon, he could see a car headed towards their house and slowly pull in the driveway. He ran to the car and there, in the back, his wife held the most beautiful dark=haired baby girl he had ever seen. Peter helped Evelyn out and then grabbed her suitcase while Bud ran ahead to open the house door for them. Peter had never met Bud before, but he seemed like a nice fellow. Bud couldn't stay, he told Peter, as he had farming to do and needed to get back. He congratulated the couple and left. Peter would never see him again nor had he ever heard from them or about them ever again. He thought to ask Evelyn about it, but she was a prickly person and he never wanted to start any conflict. For now, he was focused on his wife and this new, perfect little girl. He fell in love instantly and took part in all the parenting that comes with an infant. Evelyn was not a natural mother. She didn't seem to bond with the little girl. Peter fed her, changed her, and got up for the middle of the night feedings. He had to work but missed the little girl while he was away. Evelyn cared for the child. She met all of her needs, but she seemed distant. Marsha had called a few weeks ago and told her she had had a little baby boy and things were going really well and Bud was a wonderful father. The plan had worked and the people in the community had fallen for her fake pregnancy and her new son. It had worked just as long as no one said anything. It's a good thing Evelyn was dead; she would never know what was about to happen.

Chapter 7

Kate and Drew had a wonderful day after a wonderful morning at Borghese Park. They had seen and done all there was to do there. They got back to their room in time to take a quick nap and get ready for dinner. Italians ate late. 8 o'clock was a little early for dinner, but Kate and Drew had gotten back in time for a nap and dinner. Walking to a trattoria right down the road, they ate their fill of delicious Italian food and got back to their room full of pasta, wine, and love. Drew took his time tonight, it was like a crock pot-slow, careful, and full of the symphony that lovemaking had to offer. Kate's senses were full and alive, she couldn't remember a time where she had felt more loved, cherished, and fulfilled. Drew was like a hungry solider come back from war. She was getting braver with her inhibitions lowered due to the wine and Drew drank in her generosity.

They woke up in each other's arms and smiled at the same time. Drew pulled her against him and told her how much he loved her. She told him that as well and pushed her bottom against him. It was not possible to love another human more that she loved him in this moment. "I see I have created a wild cat," Drew said laughing sexily. "Hey, you gave me wine! I felt so relaxed with you, and I trust you! I cannot imagine loving someone more than I love you right now, Drew. I am giddy with happiness. I had a blast with you last night!"

"Woman, do you see any complaints here? I had the best day with you and gosh have you noticed that wine makes everything better?" He said laughing.

"I didn't want to think about the fact that my parents are divorcing and, honestly, I can't blame Dad. He has lived in a cold world for so long. I really hope that for the rest of his life he has nothing but love and joy in whatever form that comes in.

"I agree Kate, your dad is a nice man and has been in a dead relationship with your mom for years and I have no idea why. I am happy for him - if he will be happy. Life is too short to live with someone who is bitter towards life. You can't change anyone but yourself. I really think your dad thought that if he was kind enough to your mom she might see the light, but it's clear she chooses to be bitter and unhappy. I hope the best for him. I think he is getting close to the kids which is a good thing. He loves them. I love that he was there for the ceremony. Let's make sure we have a big bash for them after the baby in born and they have the biggest wedding. I'm all in, baby girl."

"Who are you? How do you understand so much about love and life?" Kate said looking dreamily into his eyes.

"I guess from life and the experience of loss. The Bible teaches that suffering builds character and I am full of that!!! " He said kissing the top of her head.

It was to be a glorious day. Drew had plans....and he couldn't wait.

There is a place in Rome where you can look over the whole city. At sunset, Drew brought her to this place. As the sun set on the day that his son, and now daughter-in-law married, Drew got down on one knee. The setting sun cast indescribable colors over the city, and it felt surreal.

"Kate, I believe that God has put us back together, in this time and in this place, and I want so much for you to know how much I love you and how important our family and our life together is. Kate, will you please make me the happiest man in the world and be my wife?"

Kate could not contain her overwhelming feeling of love and gratitude. She fell at Drew's feet and wept. She was truly overcome with emotion. Life had been hard for her, her childhood that was cold and unfeeling which left her wondering if she had any value at all. But Ken, and her children, had healed those wounds. And then Ken was gone, taken, ripped from her. She survived the ten years somehow, almost feeling numb to anything good. Then she took her kids advice, and moved North to her dream home, her dream spot, her dream life, and she pushed fearlessly through it. She took it. She grabbed it and she met Drew. The love of her life. The guy she had met *so* many years ago and then, because she was too young to make decisions on her own, gave her son up. All because her mother bullied her into it. It was tough to get over that. She snapped herself out of this mental video going on in her head back to the present. Here before her, kneeled a man. The man she loved, and he wanted her to spend the rest of his life with her. She looked up into those beautiful blues eyes, full of love and full of tears. "Drew, nothing would make me happier than to be your wife! I love you so much!!" With that, he slide a beautiful diamond and Sapphire ring on her finger. Blue was her favorite color, he remembered! It was not huge, as he seemed to know that she was not about bling. The ring fit perfectly, and she pulled him into a full hug so tight she thought they would lose their breath. But their breath melded together and made them one flesh. The way it was always meant to be. Just then, out of nowhere, a small group of men came out with a violin and a guitar. A man held a bottle of champagne, two glasses, and a bouquet of Zinnia's. They sang love songs to Kate and Drew while they toasted their engagement. The whole world seemed to stop, in this moment in time, to savor the moment. The full moon rose that night, the stars came out and shined over the city, life could not have been more perfect.

The next morning Kate glowed, and she kissed Drew as he pulled her next to him. They had a full day planned. They had two days left in Rome and then they would head to the Amalfi Coast. Rome was such a big city with so much to see that it could not be done in a week. To see all there was to see, you really needed to live here to see everything this incredible city had to offer.

They had to make choices on this trip and Drew really wanted to see the Catacombs. After speaking with hotel concierge who highly recommended taking the tour bus there. The transportation, there and back, could be challenging as the Catacombs of San Sebastiano were on the Via Appia Antica which was outside the walls of Rome. This would be the most efficient way to see them. The tour bus was full, as they made their way to the back of the bus where they ran into the guys from the band again! "

Hi guys! Sorry we bugged out early the other night! You guys are so fun! I hope I danced off a few the calories I've been eating since we got here!" Kate said smiling. Drew walked up and shook some of their hands and they all took their seats for the half hour ride to the Catacombs. Kate kept looking back at Tom and would catch him staring at her. Not in a creepy way but like he seemed curious, too.

The Catacombs were so interesting! Kate and Drew learned a lot. In the 300s A.D., Christians did not believe in the Pagan ritual of burning the deceased. The land, at the time, was too expensive for them to have cemeteries to bury their dead so they came up with the idea to build cemeteries underground. This particular Catacomb was about seven miles long. The people, back then, would carve out a spot in the walls of the caves and wrap their deceased loved ones in a sheet then place them in the niches in the cave wall. There were many subterranean passageways where whole families could be together. It was a little creepy as they passed skeletal remains of person after person, the sheet that had covered them long since rotted away. Kate saw many tiny remains. She asked the tour guide why so many were small babies and he told them the infant mortality rate in that century were very high.

It was good to get back out into the sunshine after being in the Catacombs for several hours. Very interesting history though. Feeling very hungry, they went back to the hotel, showered, and changed into their evening clothes. Drew had talked to the concierge again and got the name of a restaurant near the hotel they could walk to. The Pinsa e Buoi Parioli, was a charming place that did not disappoint. As they entered, they saw cured meats and cheese hanging from the ceiling and a large wall that held many bottles of wine. Small four person tables topped with white tablecloths that held small vases of flowers with real candles, created a lovely ambiance. As it was only 7 pm, very few tables were occupied. They were early for dinner. A kind, young woman came over to their table and said "American? Yes?"

Drew laughed and said, "Are we that obvious?" The young woman said "Well, Americans like to eat much earlier than we do so that gave you away. In fact, the Chef does not cook the evening meal until 8, but, I can keep you happy with a Primo, some Vino and pane. Is this suitable for you?" She spoke very good English but definitely had an accent. They both felt very grateful that they could understand her. Kate's mouth watered as the young woman set out the most wonderful bread. So crispy on the outside and soft inside. How would she ever go back home and not have this food? She liked to cook but this was at a level she couldn't imagine. She quickly checked herself for drool. Nope, still good. Next, the waitress brought out a charcuterie board which held many delights. The woman showed them a few wines and let them taste them. They decided on a lovely, dark red wine that had a lovely flavor and paired well with their starters. Drew took her hand and rubbed his thumb over ring finger. The Sapphire and diamond ring glowed in the candlelight. Kate's eyes were drawn up to Drew's which were filled with tears. "Katie, my love, I just cannot get over how blessed we are. I never thought I would find you; I had given up hope. Here you are, so beautiful, sitting in front of me and we are in Rome, Sitting in this beautiful restaurant, it all seems so incredible."

"Oh Drew, my love, I feel the same way. I think about our family back home, too, and how much in love our kids are and **we** are going to be grandparents! I am so happy for Neal and Jan. It's like our being back together has spread seeds of love everywhere and it's so wonderful to watch it grow." Kate said with a glow in her eyes.

The meal was spectacular! Afterward, they lazily walked back to the hotel pausing at the Trevi Fountain. They made their way closer, and Drew brought out a coin from his pocket and said, "You know, if you toss a coin into this fountain, it is said that you will return to Rome one day. Here wrap your hand around mine as we toss it together." Kate exclaimed, "Oh, Drew, how amazing!" They held hands and tossed the coin into the fountain where it joined the millions of other coins that held the hopes and dreams of countless others who dared to hope to come back to this magic city of love.

Chapter 8

Peter sat on the steps in front of his house with his head in his hands, weeping. He had just watched the coroner take the body of his wife out of the home they had shared for years. He should have checked on her earlier. He had tried to call her several times but, since she didn't pick up the first few days he figured she was still mad about getting the divorce papers. Then, after the kids said their vows yesterday, he thought he should stop in and tell even though, he knew, she was angry about the whole situation. Peter knew the minute he opened the front door that she was dead. The smell was overwhelming. He walked into the kitchen and saw the divorce paperwork on the counter. Then, because he was scared, he went back outside and called the police. It was mid-September, but the temperatures were still in the 80s so he wondered if anyone else had smelled the distinct odor of death. The police got there in less than ten minutes. He spoke with the kind officer about the situation that he had moved out several weeks ago and filed for divorce. Peter also told the officer that he had spoken with her, for the last time, a week ago and she had been upset, as expected. The officer took his report, then went inside and found Evelyn in her bed. It was clear what had happened, the right side of her face was in a frozen droop. The medical examiner was going to have to do an autopsy to be sure of the cause of death. You never knew, especially since the couple was going through a divorce. He gave Peter the name of a company that were experts in getting rid of the smell of death. There was no mess, no blood, just the smell of his poor wife having been in this house after death for a week. A few curious neighbors had stopped over after seeing the coroner and the police car to give their condolence. He would not share anything more other than she had passed away.

After making a call to the "smell" experts and set it up for them to come over later in the day, Peter decided to call one of his friends from church to meet at a coffee shop. It was going to take two days for the smell to go out of the house. he had arrangements to make, people to call and he felt overwhelmed. He still had his hotel room so at least that was one thing he didn't have to figure out.

Charlie stood, as he saw Peter enter the café, and went over to give him a long, tight hug and said, "So sorry, brother, to hear about your loss. Anything I can do to help? I'll be here for you in any way, I'm here for you day and night." Charlie said, as he pulled out a chair for Peter to sit in. He asked Peter what he wanted to drink and then went and got him a coffee and toast. He hadn't eaten. He didn't feel much like eating either, but he knew he had to have something to keep up the strength to do what needed to be done. "Thanks Charlie, I appreciate it, man." Peter had confided in Charlie about his marriage for the last few years. He was one of the guys in Peter's small group at church. What a blessing these men had been to him as he struggled to love a woman who was so bitter and angry about life. They had been a great source of encouragement to him. He had shared with Charlie that because of the reaction Evelyn had to their granddaughter's pregnancy, and announcement of the quick marriage, he felt that he could no longer continue on with the marriage. "I thought that when she was going to her small group with the women that she had really started to make a change in her life, and I *had* seen her soften and grow a little closer to Kate and the grandkids. But after the 4th of July celebration at Kate's, she seemed to sink back into that dark place. She ranted about how stupid it was that all these couples were getting together. I think she was jealous. She thought the fact that Neal and Jan had found love was ridiculous at their age. I must admit I felt jealous too, seeing how happy they were together, and they are the same age as me." Tears filled his eyes as he looked at his friend. "What am I going to do? Kate and Drew are in Italy for a few more weeks. Do I call and tell her or wait until they come back? I don't want to spoil things for them." Charlie reached over and patted his friend on the back. "You have to call Kate. This was her mother and no matter how things were between them; she needs to know. She has Drew with her, and she is a strong woman."

Peter nodded his head slowly, knowing he needed to call soon. It was almost 7 pm in Italy and he wanted to catch them before they went out for the evening. He thought of the itinerary they had given him and, if he was correct in remembering, they were just starting their next adventure in the Amalfi Coast. He and Charlie talked more about making the arrangements. He shared that they were doing an autopsy on her to be sure of the cause of death. It would be at least a week to hear back on that to get the body cleared for burial. Evelyn had wanted to be cremated. Peter wondered out loud if he could wait the few weeks to have a funeral for her when Kate and Drew got back from their trip. He sighed in exhaustion. So much to do and he felt a little lost. Evelyn had always taken care of everything. "We are all here for you, Peter. I can make some calls if you'd like, let the church know. As you know, there is a team of people to support you while you are going through this process. You need to know that you are not alone in this. We deeply care about you."

"You have no idea how much I needed to hear that right now. Thank you for your kindness. I think I need to go back to the hotel and rest for a while, after I call Kate."

"I will talk to the team at church and get some food sent over to you. It's the kind of food you need right now when your appetite isn't good. Remember, you will get through this, and you are not alone. Call me, day or night, if you need to talk, cry, or just need a hug. God is close to the broken hearted. He knows your situation and He is not surprised. I'll be praying for you, if you don't mind, I'll share this with the other guys in the group so they can be praying for you as well." With that the two men left the café and Peter drove the short distance to the hotel. He did feel a little better with the loving support he had gotten from Charlie. He wasn't alone. He felt a little stronger and could almost feel his friend praying for him. When he got to the room, he sat on the bed and wept. Body wracking sobs shook his body to the core. He wept for their life together that could have been full of color instead of a life of selfishness and keeping people out, the only color: gray. He held himself responsible that he had not tried harder. He should have tried to get her to talk about the path that led to her extreme unhappiness. She wasn't born angry. Anger and her bitterness had a root. He believed it was a root of rejection. He had known her parents were not loving. Like a sapling that goes without sunshine and water, her spirit had withered. He had tried so hard to love her. To show her the kind of love she had missed out on as a child. But her wound was too deep for him to reach. Her heart was too closed to receive anything good. Only God could touch that deepest part of the heart where the pain started. Only He could heal it. For a time, there was hope when she finally opened up a little to her small group. The other women had shared painful parts of their past as well. With the love, support, and acceptance from them, for a time, seemed to help. He thought because she had been this way for so long, the habit of bitterness was too hard to break; even ugly and dark provided a comfort with the familiarity of it. He shook his head in sadness. He prayed and prayed that she had made her peace with

God. It broke his heart to think she went to bed that night angry. But God is a God of love and forgiveness. He truly hoped that she was with God, finally getting the love that she had needed all her life. He got up, poured himself a large glass of water, and drank the whole thing. Taking a deep breath, he dialed Kate's number.

Drew held Kate as she finished up her call with her dad. She sat on the bed and stared out at the sea off the terrace of their beautiful room on the Amalfi Coast. They had arrived yesterday after a beautiful drive. They were exhausted from going from sunup to sundown every day in Rome and, of course, eating gallons of delicious pasta didn't help either. Drew rented a car outside of Rome and with suitcases in the trunk they made their way to a beautiful hotel on the top of a mountain. Well, in her mind it was a mountain, going round and round the switchbacks, up the large hill to a beautiful, small village. The hotel layered down and down to the beautiful beach. Drew had gotten them a spectacular room on the side of the Tyrrhenian Sea. The color of the water was sapphire and Kate thought it was the same color as Drew's eyes. They had a terrace off their room that held a table, several chairs, and large red clay pots filled with colorful flowers that draped down the sides. The view off their terrace to one side was of the sea. The other side was the mountain village that was built up with buildings and cobblestone streets throughout. The colors of each building were different and so pretty. It was like looking at a bouquet of flowers. As you looked down, off of their terrace, they could see a large rectangular pool that held majestic views of the sea and beach below. Large pots of gorgeous flowers were everywhere and a pergola off to the side where one could sit in the shade to sip wine or have a meal. They had gotten here last night, had a romantic stroll on the beach and ate the amazing seafood caught that day by the local fishermen. The fresh fish, plus the wide variety of fresh greens made for a delightful culinary journey. The fresh gelato was something Kate would never forget, and she vowed to try and figure out how to make it once she got home. It was a good to have this Heavenly view as Kate processed the news from her dad.

Her mother was dead. She had been in the house for a week without anyone having noticed. Her father wept as he shared the events of the week and how badly he felt that she had gone undetected for that long. Kate was having a hard time crying for her mother. She felt regret. Regret that she had missed so many years with her, but it was hard to be around someone all the time that was so critical, so negative, so unloving. Kate had not felt loved by her mother and, although her father had tried to fill the space where her mother left off, he was not a mother. Drew came out and rubbed her shoulders, leaned in, and kissed her neck. "Honey, I'm so sorry about your mom. I know things have been rough for a long time. I'm here when you are ready to talk, cry, get mad or whatever. I love you so much and it breaks my heart that this has happened."

"I guess the good part about this is that we had found a little peace in the last few months since she had the mini stroke. I think with more time, maybe we could have grown closer. But we will never know now. I just feel so bad that my dad is there alone. He did mention a great support group through his church so that makes me feel better. I know Addie said that he had been around a lot more with them and has reached out and expressed the desire to be closer with them. I'll call Addie and see if they can go and spend some time with him. Dad said there is to be an autopsy and that will take a week or so and that Mom wanted to be cremated. He said we are **not** to cut our trip short. But I don't know -it seems wrong to be happy right now and in this beautiful place when my poor dad is going through this."

"Kate, honey, we can be on a plane tomorrow if you want to go and be there with your dad. I will do whatever you need to do." He said rubbing her arm gently.

"Why can't I cry? It feels like I should be crying! Am I horrible?"

"Of course, you are not horrible!!! You have been grieving the loss of your mother for years! Almost since the time you were born! You grew in the understanding year by year that she was never going to be the kind of mother that you needed. I heard once that you can't give what you don't have. She didn't have it to give. I feel bad that whoever hurt your mother, caused her to choose a loveless life. She had a choice. Your father loved her and was good to her but deep down her pain ate who she was meant to be. You're a great example of someone who longed for a mother who couldn't be what you needed, and you became that mother for your children. With the help of God, your faith, and some good people in your life, you just made different choices than she did. It's so sad really. She pushed everyone away that might love her so she wouldn't get rejected. She's with God now. Let that bring you some peace, my love. You can move forward and have a closer relationship with your dad now."

"How did you get so smart Drew? I feel like you have hit the nail right on the head with everything you just said. I feel like I just had a great therapy session." She stood and they held each other tightly. She began to weep, for her mother, her father, and the little girl inside her that would never get what she had always longed for from her mother. She thanked God for Jan, who had seamlessly stepped into that role. But it wasn't the same. It was too late to call Addie so she would call her first thing tomorrow -it would be in the afternoon then, when she was done with her teaching job. Gosh, so many things had happened since they were gone. Kate felt the pull to go home and fix everyone and everything. But she couldn't change anything. Death waited for no one, and it was never convenient. Kate looked at Drew while he got things settled in the room, keeping busy to give her some space but also right there in case she needed him. "Hey honey," she said walking toward the drawers he had just filled, "Let's go and take a swim. That will be so relaxing, and we both love it. For right now, with the time change, there is nothing we can do today. For now, I want to stay, but I'll talk to Dad again tomorrow and we can make some plans then."

"Sounds like a good plan, Katie love." They changed into their suits and made their way down the steps to the gorgeous pool. It was going to be 86 today and Kate could not wait to let the sunshine warm her heart and soul while she grieved.. There weren't many people here as Italians usually vacationed in August to the south of France and Southern Spain to get away from the heat. The pool had a few others, but it was quiet and mellow. They grabbed some nice chairs to float in and a waiter brought them some refreshing drinks to sip as they floated soaking up the sun. She prayed while she floated, and she laid it all at His feet. This always helped her when she felt overwhelmed. She didn't have to carry the burden alone. Kate realized that she had forgotten to tell her father that she was now engaged. But the timing was not right; she would wait until she got home.

Kate hung up after talking with her dad the next morning. He had told her to please stay. It was going to take some time for everything to be arranged with the autopsy and the cremation. He planned for a memorial service a few days after Kate and Drew were due back. Kate worried about him going through all of this alone, but he said he had a great group of guys from church that had circled the wagons around him. He said Neal had called him and invited him to come to his place for a few days to relax, do some fishing, and hang out with a fellow widower. Kate's heart was warmed at how generous and kind Neal was being with her dad. That definitely made her feel better about staying. Addie and Joe invited him for dinner, and he had gotten lots of hugs and support from them as well. Harry had gone to the house after the fans were done doing their job. He and Peter had long talks. Peter was thrilled at the growing relationships with his grandchildren. At night when he was alone, the guilt set in, and he would cry and grieve that Evelyn missed out on so much in her life. But then he would fall into a fitful sleep. When the sun came up everything seemed better. He was packing a bag to head to Neal's place for a few days and he was really looking forward to hanging out and getting to know him better.

Drew put on golf shorts and a sleeveless black shirt while Kate put on a sundress and some comfortable sandals, both getting ready for their day in the village. It was about a mile walk along the narrow cobblestone streets. Small shops were everywhere along the streets including open markets with fresh fruits and vegetables, meats and cheeses strung up and fresh flower stands. There was a man selling beautiful rugs that they stopped by to look at . Next to that was a shop that had gorgeous hand-painted Italian pottery. Kate fell in love with a set and wanted so much to buy it, but she couldn't figure out how she would get it back to the States. She was thrilled when the shop owner, who spoke some English, told her she could have it shipped back to the home. It would take a little time, but it could be done. She bought some lovely wine glasses to go with the pottery set as well.

They stopped for lunch at a little trattoria. Kate ordered a salad with mixed greens, nibbled on the delicious bread that came with every meal, and dipping it into the olive oil. Drew ordered some pasta carbonara, which is a fantastic pasta made with raw eggs and pancetta. When her salad came, Kate looked down in horror. There were plenty of mixed greens alright, but the outside of the bowl was decorated with small Octopus legs all the way around. It made Kate think of spiders. Kate was an Arachnophobe. Drew was served his pasta and saw the look on Kate face. "Honey what is it? What wrong?"

"Drew, there are tentacles on my bowl- I can't do this."
She said, her eyes focused on the sky.

"Here, let me take them off for you" Kate loved that he
didn't make her feel bad or foolish about this even
though it might seem silly to him. Kate watched as
Drew tried to pull the Octopus legs off the bowl but the
suckers on the legs stuck. He probably could have
picked the bowl up using the legs as handles! Ew! Kate
paled. Drew took the dish, stood up, walked over to the
waiter, and apologized; asking if she could order
another dish please. The waiter didn't really understand
but he went and found the owner who did speak some
English. Drew said that she changed her mind about
what she wanted, and it was no big deal. He then made
his way back to the table where Kate was drinking her
wine......really fast. "Sorry I am such a baby about
that! I feel so dumb, but I hate how that looked! It was
like a big spider on the plate! Plus, who garnishes a
plate with Octopus' legs?!"

"Don't worry honey, we all have our weird stuff and
that's just yours. Mine is that I hate chunks of tomato in
sauces, and I cannot eat pudding without gagging. So
there ya go!" Kate ordered a lovely piece of fish that
came with rosemary roasted potatoes. She would skip
the salad today.

It was getting very warm, so they decided to walk back
to the hotel for a walk down the beach and perhaps
swim. When they got down there, they found a small

boat tour they could take; it would only take two hours to tour the vicinity. It was so lovely out and it gave them a unique view of the village and hotel from the sea. The sea was calm, and you could almost see down to the bottom where the fish were colorful and plentiful. The sea was a stunning azure blue today. Tomorrow, they planned to make the hour drive to see the city of Pompeii. Mount Vesuvius had covered the city in ash and killed more than 2000 people around 79 A.D. They planned to leave early and be back by mid-afternoon so they could rest and have lunch.

Chapter 9

Neal brought Peter another beer and joined him on the screen porch at his home on Goose Lake. It was a warm September evening. Neal made them steaks on the grill, nuked some potatoes, and made a salad. He wouldn't let Peter do anything but help carry the food outside where then men now sat chatting." Neal, I don't think you know this, but I had moved out of the house and had asked Evelyn for a divorce. It had been coming for years really, but I just stayed because I took my vows seriously. She had become consumed with bitterness, hatred, and spewed her venom anywhere she could. I really thought that I could love her, and it would help some, but it seemed to get worse after Jake came into the picture. It wasn't his fault of course! But it set something off in her and I don't know why. She never opened up to me much. I know she had it rough as a kid, but she wasn't abused or anything that I know of. I've known her all my life!"

"I had no idea, Peter! I knew Kate had been estranged from you guys because of the adoption. That's about all I knew. Evelyn seemed to be pleasant on the 4th of July. I am so sorry that things turned out this way. I know you spoke of your men's group through church, man. they got me through some dark days after my wife died. And even though you were seeking a divorce, you still had a life together and a child. I'm here for you - anytime."

"Thanks! Harry has been great. He and Addie are coming over in a few days to help me go through her things and decide what to do with them. They really are great kids. Kate and Ken did a fine job raising those kids. Such a damn shame when Ken passed away. We were not close with Kate then. I feel terrible about all the years lost. You can't ever get them back, can you?" Peter said with sad eyes.

"The only thing you can do is move forward and change how you do things now Pete. Regret is pointless. You have time left to spend with Kate and her kids. Drew is a terrific guy, and I couldn't be more pleased that they found each other again."
"I agree. Ken was a tough act to follow but Drew is one heck of a guy! "

"Let's go fishing, if want to talk more then we will and if you want to just ponder, you can do that too. Fishing to me makes everything better."

"That sound great, Neal."

Off the two men went to fish, to ponder, to talk a little. They caught many fish that night and Peter finally slept well. After a few days of relaxing with Neal, he needed to get back to the house as he was meeting with Harry and Addie. Jan had come to have dinner with them last night. She had been working at the grocery store so

Neal could hang out with Peter. She was a wonderful woman and Peter wondered if he would ever find anyone who would love him.

" Hey Grandpa, how about we make a few piles - keep, throw, and give away? I don't want to hurry you in any way. I want you to go at your own pace. I'm sure this isn't going to be easy, but we are both here for you." Addie said while sitting on the chair in the master bedroom.

"Well, I guess we should start with her clothes. I don't' know much about that stuff. Maybe you can go through them and put most of them in the donate pile and the stuff that is worn, torn, or outdated we can just put in the trash. Is that okay with you? I am going to start working on the kitchen. Let me know if you need me for anything." He said as he left the bedroom.

"Sounds good to me." Addie said and gave him a hug.

Addie made fairly short work of going through her grandmothers' clothes. She had some decent things and was able to put quite a bit in the donate pile. She got rid of most of the shoes that were too worn but there were several that someone else might get some use from. It wasn't hard because Evelyn was practically a stranger.

So, there was very little emotional attachment with her things. She was getting the last of the shoes off the floor when her fingernail caught on a piece of loose wood from the floor. The splinter went deep under her fingernail causing her to yelp. "OUCH!" She was hopping around saying "Owie, owie, owie!"

"What happened?" Harry asked as he rushed into the room. He had been assigned to another area of the house.

"Oh, I caught my nail on some loose wood in the floor of the closet. Here, can you pull it out?" He was able to then she washed it carefully in the sink in the bathroom. When she came back in, she saw Harry kneeling on the floor of the closet. He was trying to see if he could fix it so it wouldn't happen again. "Hey look! The floorboard is loose!" Harry gave it a gentle pull and the whole piece came out! He was sure there would be buried treasure in there. He was not disappointed when he stuck his hand in and pulled out an old cigar box. "Wow, Addie, look at this! Should we open it? I wonder if it's been here longer than Grandpa and Grandma owned the house?" Addie went over as Harry stood with the very old box. They opened it slightly and saw an old diary and some papers. "Um, I think we better get Grandpa." Addie went down to the kitchen where Peter was making some sandwiches for lunch. Harry followed after her and told him what he had found and how.

"Really?! Let's see it. "Peter said as he took the box and sat down at the kitchen table. "Help yourself to some sandwiches, kids. He gently opened the box and saw a diary. He opened and saw that it was Evelyn's handwriting. It was from a long time ago, dated around the same year Kate was born. For now, he'd set that aside and looked through the other things in the box. Strange there were a stack of letters from her cousin Marsha. He hadn't thought about her in years! He looked up and saw the kids staring at him in anticipation. "Uh, It's nothing really. An old diary of Evelyn's and some letters from a distant cousin she used to hang out with a long time ago." He put everything back in the box and set it aside. He would read it later in private. The kids were disappointed, but this was his private business.

The rest of the day the kids helped in any way possible. Harry brought all the bags of the giveaway stuff in the back of his truck. He would drop it all off at Good Will on his way home. He saw the look on his grandfather's face as he took the last traces of his wife's clothing outside. Like a puff of mist, gone. Our time on Earth was so fast. He shook his head in grief and walked back into the house. Addie hugged him and set a nice dinner in front of him. She needed to get going. She was exhausted after all the work they had done and just wanted to go home and put her swollen feet up. "Thanks so much, kiddo, for all of your help! I couldn't have done it without you guys." Harry had come back in and also gave him a hug. "We're here for you,

Gramps. Call anytime. If there is more that you need help with - give me a shout. Are you going to be okay here tonight? I know it's your first night back in the house......I can stay if you want." Harry stated. "No, you kids go on home now. I need to do this first night alone and I have my small group of guys I can call too. But I'm doing ok, really. Love you kids." After giving him another hug, he watched as his grandkids left. Wow, what great kids. He loved spending time with them after so many years of being shut out. He held onto Neal's words about no regrets. He needed to stay in the present. It's all any of us have. The right now.

Peter pulled out a TV table then turned on the TV to catch up on the news while he ate the meatloaf, baked potato, and steamed broccoli Addie made for him. She had made cupcakes as well. What a sweet girl - he thought as he ate. It was delicious. After he ate, he washed his dishes and put them in the dish drain to dry.

Eyeballing the box, he picked it up, took it back into the living room and sat in his favorite chair. He opened the box and took out the diary. Was it wrong to read it? Evelyn had hidden it for a reason. But in the end, he decided to read it. It might give him some insight as to why she was the way she was. It grew dark in the room, and he had to turn on the lamp beside him as he read page after page of her diary. He finished several hours later and just stared at the picture of them on the mantel above the fireplace. He stood, walked over to the picture, and picked it up. His hands shook and he spoke to the picture of his wife. "WHY? WHY? WHY would you *do* this?? How could you do this to us? TO ME? TO HIM???" He angrily threw the picture against the wall, and it shattered into a million pieces just like his heart. He fell to the floor and wept like he never had before. His body wracked with the terrible pain of grief. He whimpered over and over. "How could you? How could you? How could you?" After what seemed like hours, he got up off the floor, went into the kitchen and poured himself a large shot of bourbon. With shaky hands, he went back in and sat in his chair. He picked out the letters and began to read. A photo fell out of one of the letters and it was a picture of a boy who looked to be about 12. He was the spitting image of Kate-his sister. Her twin brother. Evelyn would have kicked herself for saving this box all these years. But she was dead and didn't know. He downed the bourbon, got up, and got another one. It hit him like a ton of bricks. He had a son. He was raised by Marsha and Bud. He had read all about the plot, the dirty doctor, the scam of her going there early to have his babies and the plan to give his son away. She wrote in her diaries that she hadn't wanted children at all. But just to keep him happy she'd keep one. How did she decide? Eeny, meeny, miny, moe? He had a 53-year-old son. He looked at the clock, it was 2 am. Peter dragged himself up to the room he had shared with his lying wife for all these years. He set his glass down and tore the blankets off the bed. He looked then at her dresser that held her brush and her perfumes and he violently wiped them off with one swipe of his arm. He picked up a pillow and screamed as loud as he could into it. He was furious! He would never sleep in this room again, in fact, tomorrow this house of lies would go on the market - or as soon as he could get rid it. He went to the linen closet in the hall, grabbed some blankets, and took them to the spare room. There was a small bed in the room where on nights that he couldn't sleep, he would come to this room. Peter lay there all night long trying to figure out what he was going to do. The next morning, he went back downstairs and made a big pot of coffee. Leaning against the counter, he called his friend, Charlie, from church. "You said I could call anytime. Can you please come over? I need to talk."

To which Charlie responded, "I'm on my way, give me ten minutes." While Peter waited, he cleaned up the broken mess in the living room.

"What?!" Charlie asked, stunned, after Peter told him what he found out last night. "This sounds like the stuff from a bad movie! What are you going to do? Can you press charges against the couple that took the baby? It was not legal at all and the doctor!! How devastating!"

∞∞∞∞∞∞∞∞∞∞∞∞∞∞∞∞∞∞∞∞∞∞∞∞∞∞∞∞∞∞∞∞∞∞∞∞

Neal and Jan sat out on the deck by the fire pit on an early evening in mid-September and talked about their wedding plans. Both wanted a small affair with just close friends and family. They planned to marry at the church, in a small afternoon ceremony, on Christmas Eve. then have people back to Neal's house afterwards. It had been decided that Jan would sell her home on Cedarcrest Lake and move in with Neal. Jan loved Neal's place, it didn't matter to her that his wife had decorated it and had her stamp on it. Jan felt very at home there. They would, however, get a new bed and new linens. Best to start a marriage with a new bed! Drew expressed an interest in buying her lake cabin. He wanted a place where all the kids could come up to stay and until he and Kate got married, Drew could live there. It was a great idea as she would not have the headache of putting her place on the market. Jan looked around her house and other than photos and some personal things, she really had no trouble selling it to Drew furnished. She and her husband had taken very good care of the place and prior to his death, they had made some necessary updates. It was a few months before the wedding so she would have time to go through things and decide what she wanted to keep.

Both Jan and Neal were free to talk about the marriages they had with their deceased spouses. They had both had really good marriages. Like all marriages, they had gone through their tough times but had persevered through them. For Jan, the hardest part had been that despite years of trying, no children came. Neal and Jan were both from the school of thought that you didn't become intimate until you were married. They were both in their early 70's, what made it beautiful was that they got to delve really deep emotionally. There were no games played, just openness and honesty. Neal was such a kind man. They had so much fun together! When he bought the grocery store, Jan thought she might not see him much, but to her surprise, he asked her to work there with him. She worked in the office and was brilliant at customer service. They had hired competent people so that they didn't have to spend many days or hours at the store. They would stop in three mornings a week to see how things were going with the staff and the store. She would get some work done in the office while Neal chatted with the temporary manager to make sure everything was going ok. His grandson, Sam, was getting out of the military soon and he wanted to offer him the job overseeing the whole business. Sam expressed interest in this and was excited to have something to come home to. Luckily, Sam had worked mostly Stateside. He was turning 32 soon and was ready to find a wife and have a family. Neal told him there were some really nice gals at the church and a really cute blond that worked at the pharmacy in the next town. Sam told his grandfather to hold off on the matchmaking until he got home. They had always been close and got along great. For now, Jan was excited about a new and unexpected chapter in her life. It had changed so much! She was now going to have a big family! The thought of Christmas shopping for everyone made her dizzy with excitement. Addie was going to have a baby in January, so it would be like being a real great grandmother! She felt so blessed and thankful. She had felt sad the other night when Peter was at Neal's. The poor man suddenly losing his wife. She hoped Kate was doing okay in Italy hearing the news. Kate had shared a lot with Jan about the lack of relationship she'd had with her mother and the reasons why. But after her mother had a small stroke, they had at least forgiven each other. No good hanging on to the past. She knew she could never take the place of a mother, but if she had a daughter? She would be cherished, and she cherished Kate.

∞∞∞∞∞∞∞∞∞∞∞∞∞∞∞∞∞∞∞∞∞∞∞∞∞∞∞∞∞∞∞∞∞∞∞∞∞∞∞

Peters' friend left after hugging him. As soon as he saw him pull of out the driveway, he got right in his car and drove to Marsha and Bud's house in Wisconsin. It took him 45 minutes. He got out of the car and walked right up to the back door and knocked loudly. A young woman in her twenties, he guessed, swung the door open. "Yes what can I do for you?"

"I'm sorry to bother you, some relatives of mine used to live here. Do you know where Marsha and Bud are?"

Just then a man came up behind the woman and opened the door wider saying "Hey, can I help you? "

"Uh yes I was just telling this young woman that some relatives of mine used to live here. I have some news to share, and this is the last place they lived." Nodding the young man told him they had bought the house a year ago from Bud and Marsha. He said he had heard that Bud passed away and that Marsha was living with her sister in a four-plex in town. "Let me see if I have the forwarding address, I did a while back when she was still getting mail here, can you wait, please?" Peter nodded and thanked the man. The woman stood there in the doorway looking at him. "Who did you say you are?" She asked looking him up and down. "Oh, I'm sorry, my name is Peter Spencer. My wife's cousin is Marsha, my wife just passed away and I wanted to give her the news in person. They were very close a long time ago." Just then, her husband came back and handed him a card. "I copied the address down for you, but I don't have a phone number. It's just on the other side of town over the bridge." Peter reached out for the card and then shook his hand. "Thanks, you've been a great help" and with that he turned and went back to the car.

On the drive over, Peter wondered how he was going to do this. He was still so mad. But he was determined to expose the truth and find his son. True to his word, the young man was correct, it was a quick drive as he pulled up in front of the brick four- plex. He slowly got out of the car. He walked up to the building and saw the buttons on the side with the names of the people living there. He didn't see her name but the other names were all married couples, so he rang the buzzer for the other one that had two last names listed that were different. He waited. "Hello? Who is there?"

"Hi, this is Peter Spencer; I'm looking for Marsha?"

"Peter? What on Earth are you doing here? Let me buzz you in." With that, the door buzzed and unlocked. He walked up to the second floor and knocked. Marsha opened the door and invited Peter in. "Hello Marsha, long time- no see, in fact, the last time I saw you Evelyn was pregnant. She passed away last week. I thought you should know. She also left behind a diary and some letters from you."

Marsha paled and slowly sat down. "So, you know........."

"Yes, I damn well know! Now where is my son!"

Marsha was shaking like a leaf. She had dreaded this day for 53 years. She had prayed it wouldn't come at least until they had raised the boy. She had almost believed after all these years that the secret would never be found out. "Peter, I know it was wrong, but at the time, we all thought it was a good plan. Evelyn didn't want the children. She was determined once she found out she was having twins to get rid of one and we had been trying for years to have a child. We have cherished him and loved him with all our hearts."

"DOES HE KNOW?" Peter was trying to control his anger, but he was shaking. Marsha started to cry. Her head down in shame. "No, he doesn't know. Bud died last year and took it to his grave. Thomas is in Italy right now with his band. They are on a tour. He won't be home for another week." Peter took a seat in a chair across from Marsha. "Are you kidding me? My daughter Kate, HIS SISTER is in Italy on a trip. What if they run into each other?" He rubbed his head in frustration and fear.

"Peter, she has no idea about Thomas, even if they did run into each other, they have no knowledge about one another." Peter stood and paced, Marsha got up and went into the other room and when she got back, she held a large stack of photo albums. With tears rolling down his face, Peter turned page after page of his son's life.. It broke his heart that he had missed out on his life. His grief overcame him, and he sobbed. Marsha wept along with him and at some point, she got up and soon he felt a glass put into his hands. It held some amber liquid, and he drank it in one gulp. She stood by sipping hers. "What are you going to do?" She asked sitting back down.

"I want to know where this doctor is, what he did was so illegal! "

"He's dead, he died 30 years ago, drank himself to death." So, no one would pay for this crime. His wife gone, Bud, gone, the doctor gone, only this shell of a woman sat before him. What good would it do for the woman who raised his son to be in jail? "I'll tell you what I'm going to do, when he gets back from Italy you, me and Kate are going to have a sit down and you are going to tell the truth. If you don't want to be part of that, they will get all of the truth from me through Evelyn's diary and the letters you wrote to her. I **will** meet my son. He will know that I am his father and Kate is his twin sister. Whatever time we have left will be as a family. What you did was horrible and wrong." Marsha wept. She wiped her nose on the tissue she had in her pocket. "Please try and understand, we thought this was a bad situation that we could make good. We would get a child that we so desperately wanted, and Evelyn would get a child, too. I'm sorry, we didn't really think at the time about how this might affect you. If you didn't know, it wouldn't hurt you. We were selfish."

"I really don't want to hear one more word from you. I want to press charges against you for kidnapping! That's how angry I am. That's what you did! You kidnapped my son! But you are an old woman now and you will have to live with the consequences of the terrible choice you made back then. I hope MY son can forgive you, but right now, I don't care about you at all." With that, he stood up walked out the door, and slammed it as hard as he could. He would not tell anyone about this other than his church friends until Kate got back. Then the #$%^&*^% would hit the fan.

Chapter 10

The drive to Pompeii was glorious! Drew took the curves slowly down the mountain village road and followed the GPS on his phone to the other side of the spur where Pompeii was. They could see Mount Vesuvius off in the distance. It was, still to this day, an active volcano and the 3 million people who lived below the it were in great danger every day for another disaster. Reading up on it, she saw that a large eruption was due; what would happen to all the people living there now? Arriving in time for the 10 am tour, they walked around the town that in 79 A.D had been buried by volcanic ash and toxic gas. Even though it had been so many years ago, you could see the bodies that were frozen in time, covered in what had been ash but has now turned to stone. How sobering, Kate thought, as she peered inside people's homes. Bodies lay here and there; some you could tell were parents laying over their children trying to protect them. Kate had read that a lot of the town's people had left when they felt the rumblings of the Earth underground. Being so close to the sea, Pompeii had been a bustling town, filled with both rich and poor, merchants and filled taverns, fisherman and travelers On the fateful afternoon, in late summer or early fall, those that chose to stay behind, it is thought that the number around 2,000, met their fate on that day. It had been violent and those that stayed were insured almost instant death as the wall of ash and toxic air took them out. Kate could see over the town in the distance the ever-looming mountain. It looked so beautiful from here. But like Mount St. Helens, looks can be deceiving. Some poor attempts early on at excavating Pompeii did not go well. They lacked proper tools and it wasn't until the 1900's that a better job of excavation of this site was started. In the 1970s, they really got in there with the right tools with the right professionals and got it done properly. It was said that because this city was just a normal city, and not like the city of Naples, that they didn't want to bother with the excavation of Pompeii because there were not the riches that would have been found in a bigger city. No big caches of jewelry for instance. It wasn't until they began to uncover this city, that had been covered for 16oo years, they discovered that it was quite a historical archeological find. The city had been so perfectly preserved under the ash. It was easy to see how this city looked. The shops, the people, and the homes they lived in. It is still, to this day, one of the most well-preserved cities in the world. What an interesting day! They were actually walking on streets that were well over 2000 years old. Drew loved history and he was eating it all up. The amphitheater was still perfectly intact, the forum stood proudly and held its secrets in its walls. The Italian government had to step in a few years ago to protect and restore Pompeii as it had been mismanaged; a lot of looting had taken place. It was so fascinating to see this city and how it had looked so many years ago. This was one of her favorite things so far. But she seemed to say that about everything she saw here. Drew loved it too and after the several hour tour, they drove back along the coast.

On the way to the hotel, Kate thought of her mother and wondered how her dad was doing. She still felt bad being here when he was back home and grieving. But he said he had plenty of people around and his church group had circled the wagons. As if reading her mind, Drew reached over and held her hand. "I'm starving! Let's go get some food! "Kate laughed to herself, maybe not. She smiled warmly at him and agreed that it was time to get something to eat. They got back to their room and freshened up. Drew suggested they get into their suits and go down by the pool to eat there. Kate thought this was a wonderful idea and they made their way down to the poolside. They had a lovely light lunch of mixed greens with roasted garbanzo beans and some lovely fresh herbs. Drew got a ricotta stuffed ravioli and they shared. Italians shut things down in the afternoon for about three hours during the hottest hours of the day after their midday meal which then led to a time of napping. Things would open back up around 4pm until around 9 pm which was the time Italians ate their dinner. Drew and Kate lounged by the pool and swam and then thought it might be a good idea to go back to the room for a nap too.

Soon they would go to the villa in Tuscany for two weeks. It had been a nice, restful week here after the busy schedule they had in Rome.

Back at home, it was moving day for Addie. Joe had helped her pack up her things and hired a truck and movers to help. He lived in a nice condo and there was plenty of room. The plan was to finish out his lease in June and then buy a house. Both loved the country, small-town living but the commute to their jobs would be long. They needed to figure out where they wanted to live but in the meantime this would be perfect. There was room for the baby, too! She was getting excited and now that the drama at school was over, they could get on with their lives. Addie had a wedding to plan, too. She was really starting to miss her mom, and she would *still* be gone for another two weeks. Addie hadn't realized until now how much she relied on her mother's advice and support until now. She felt particularly vulnerable now that she was pregnant. It wasn't like "I need my Mommy!" It was more like "I really want to share this with Mom." Addie was unpacking a container that held her shoes and opened the large closet in the master bedroom. When she did, an avalanche of clothes nearly knocked her over! Joe walked in right at this time and was met with raised eyebrows and her mouth in a giant O. "Uh, yeah......sorry, I am a bit of a packrat. I have clothes in there from ten years ago. I just haven't taken the time to go through it." Addie thought, ugh - day 1 of living with my husband. She backed up and just sat on the bed. She didn't have the energy right not to tackle a huge job like this. He went over and knelt by her and said "Honey, I have another bedroom with an empty closet, let's put your things in there for now, and then as soon as I can, tackle this job and make room for your things in here."

"But Joe, the other room is for the baby!" She said looking at him forlornly. "Honey the baby is not due for five months. I'll have it done this weekend! I'm so sorry honey, we have just been so busy that I didn't get to it yet." She looked away and rolled her eyes. She didn't feel like herself. It felt like the hormones had taken over her body and she was the crabby version of herself. She hated that. Normally, things didn't get to her but it seemed like everything got to her now. UGH! She hoped she would go back to being herself once the baby was born. "Sorry honey, I don't feel like myself right now, I feel like I'm crabby all the time. I was just thinking I hope to get back to feeling like myself after the baby is born, sorry you live with a crab."

"Honey, why don't you give yourself a break! You have had a lot of your plate lately. The pregnancy, the problems with your job that led us to speed up our wedding, your mom not being here and then on top of our moving in together, your grandmother passed away suddenly. Come on, let's leave this mess for later, in fact, while you are having a cup of tea, with your feet up, I'll go clean out the closet while you rest, and tonight, we can finish getting your clothes put away. You're not in this alone, sweetie, I'm right here! I know you're a strong woman, but now you have me, and I'm not going to let you go through any of this alone, ok?" He leaned in and brought her up off the bed and gave her a long and tender hug, grabbing her hand he led her downstairs, got her situated on the couch, grabbed a book for her and made her a perfect cup of tea. I mean, really? Who was this wonderful man she married! She felt so blessed! Instead of getting frustrated with her, he gave her what she needed. While she rested on the couch with her feet up, a comfy blanket covering her with a perfect cup of tea, she thought of her mom who always said a good cup of tea makes everything better....and she was right. She smiled thinking of her mom and Drew in Italy. Oh, the adventures they must be having! Kate hoped that once she had the baby *and* a real wedding, that she and Joe would be able to get away for a honeymoon. She knew her mom would love to watch the baby when they went. She hoped when that time came, she would be able to leave the little bundle of joy for a bit. She and had Joe decided not to know the sex of the baby before. She liked the idea of a surprise.

∞∞∞∞∞∞∞∞∞∞∞∞∞∞∞∞∞∞∞∞∞∞∞∞∞∞∞∞∞∞∞∞∞∞∞

Jake and Jenna were settling nicely into their home and were anxious to start their new lives together. Jake had heard that his grandmother had passed away but since he barely knew her, it hadn't really didn't affected him emotionally. He would go to the funeral, however, had heard that nothing would be done until Drew and Kate got back from Italy. Jenna loved setting up her new home and in the fenced in backyard there was room for her to dig out a garden. Jake rented a tiller and got it all set to go for her. It was the wrong time of year to plant anything, but it would be ready for her in the spring. Jake felt like he had known Jenna forever. They enjoyed getting to know each other more and more. Jake was a great guy and Jenna was a sweetie. His dog, Whiskey, adored Jenna! He had a mom! It was a good match all around. They had talked before about having children and because she was in her early 30s, they both felt like sooner rather than later was a good idea. They had discussed this before they got married and Jenna hoped that soon she would have wonderful news for her husband. She was already a few days late in getting her period but wanted to wait a little longer before she got a pregnancy test. She didn't want to steal Addie's thunder. Jake had a great job and earned a very decent living. He really wanted Jenna to be able to take as much time as she needed and wanted after the children came. He had been saving money, living on his own for years, and had a nice nest egg set aside. Jenna was still paying off her student loans and would be for a while. Jake was great at finances as was she, and when they moved in together, she sold her condo and had gotten a good price for it. This profit would go into helping pay off some of her loans.

Jenna loved to fly and had only been at it for two years so she was not ready to give that up just yet. She thought maybe she might take six months off after the baby was born and then, get back to flying. Jake was completely supportive. There was something comforting about being in your 30s and doing all of this. All the childishness was out of their systems, and both knew who they were. They were so tickled to get a 'save the date' from Neal and Jan. They would be getting married on Christmas Eve! How romantic!!! Just a small wedding at their church, with close friends and family for a reception at Neal and Jan's home. Jan was selling her house to Drew and was going to keep it available for family to stay in. Jenna *loved* being part of this big family! It was also lovely to know the parents that raised him. His mother was so lovely. Jake also had a younger brother named Mike and a sister named Angela. They were a close-knit family as well. They had invited them over soon after she moved in and decided then that twice a month family game night would be scheduled. It had been a huge success. Jenna's family was from Texas, and although they were close, she didn't get down there too often. If she happened to get a flight to Texas, she was able to stop in and see them. Her dad had a cattle ranch that had been in the family for generations. Her mother had been a schoolteacher. Her mother had always had horses and loved her life on the ranch. She opened the ranch up to people with disabilities and allowed groups to come to the ranch to ride horses. It was very fulfilling. Her dad continued to ranch with Jenna's brother, James. She called him Jaime but as he got older, he preferred to be called JJ. His real name was John James. Her family had come up for their tiny wedding and loved Jake. Jenna's father had put Jake through the ringer a little. After all, she was his baby girl. But he saw that Jake had great character and he knew his Jenna. She was a strong woman just like her mother. I mean she was flying airplanes!!! He could not be prouder of his daughter. Jenna gushed as she thought of her family. If she WAS pregnant, her mother would be over the moon happy. Jenna got up and walked into the 3rd bedroom of Jake's condo, it was totally empty; she thought this might make the perfect nursery. There was so much to celebrate this year and she could not believe how blessed she was with her new life. She thought flying was the best thing she had ever done, but she thought that meeting Jake was the icing on the cake of her life. Life indeed was good!

Chapter 11

Kate and Drew were in love with the Amalfi Coast. Every day, they took a day trip to the surrounding towns and had lunch, explored the town, and met amazing people from all over the world. They laughed and cried at some of the stories other travelers had experienced. They met another couple from Florida who were on a second honeymoon. They were new empty nesters and needed to rekindle their relationship and Italy was just the romantic place to do this. Their time here was coming to an end and Kate was looking forward to going to Tuscany. There were so many things to see there! Florence, Pisa, and the vineyards. They had been told by locals that the bigger towns were very touristy and if they wanted a taste of real Tuscany, to venture outside of Florence and Pisa. There were delightful discoveries to be made. Yahoo!

Drew shook his head as Kate bought another suitcase. She was slowly filling it with things to bring back. Gifts for the kids, some clothes (she was obsessed with the Italian clothes!) and she bought two new pair of shoes in Rome on the famous shopping street, the Via Veneto. Drew had made a few purchases as well, but he, of course, didn't bring as much as Kate. The hotel had a laundry facility, so she was able to wash all of their clothes for the next two weeks of their trip. Italy was not a large country, so their drive to Tuscany would only take about three hours. Drew had rented a small villa there close to the region of Chianti.

The drive there was incredible and took much longer than three hours as Kate needed to stop frequently to take pictures. He loved the memories they were creating. Since Kate loved to cook, the locals wanted them to make sure to get some Tuscany Oil, it was said to be the best, and the only place you could get it was Tuscany. There was another region they needed to travel to, as well, for the white truffles. This next adventure was going to be a LOT about the food. Drew had set up a surprise cooking class for Kate at the Villa Bordoni. It was a 17th century family villa that had been owned by the Bordoni family, a family of wealthy merchants from Florence. It had been purchased and re-made into a hotel and restaurant. The surrounding grounds were gorgeous, landscaped gardens.

It is a hilly country and Montefili Vineyard was at the top of the hill. There, they made wonderful, rich SanGiovese wines. With the unique soil of packed clay and limestone, it created an incredible wine. Drew planned for them to tour the vineyard.

Drew had also arranged for them to go horseback riding through the region and they could also rent Vespa's. He was really excited about all these surprises he had in store for her. Kate was just like a child, you could almost see her as a little girl, excited and running with her tongue hung out as she asked him to stop again for another picture. She didn't want just landscape, he had to be in all the pictures with her. She said, over and over, how she was tracking their trip in photos, and she didn't want to forget one moment. Finally, they got to their little villa. They pulled into an old looking farmhouse. It wasn't like a farmhouse in the States, but the little villa was made of stucco and stone. It was very charming on the outside with window boxes full of beautiful flowers. As they entered, they both stopped and gasped in surprise. With wood beamed ceilings, the living room had big overstuffed white couches, a stone fireplace, and a rustic kitchen with dried flowers and herbs hanging from nails. Through French doors was a lovely intimate patio that had a small fire pit that led out to a kidney shaped pool surround by well-manicured bushes. Luxurious lounge chairs with comfortable, white cushions with small tables in between. Large urns here and there were overflowing with a kaleidoscope of colors. Flowers of which she had never seen!. Both still held their breath as they looked around at what was to be their 'home' for the next two weeks. "Oh Drew!! I think I have died and gone to Heaven!!" He came up behind her and put his arms around her waist. "I don't think I ever want to leave, Kate; I believe we *are* in Heaven! Wow!! I don't know what to do first! Did you check out the herbs in the kitchen? It smells amazing in there!" They walked back into the kitchen. On the sideboard was a spread of fresh crunchy ciabatta bread, several kinds of cheeses, beautiful Mediterranean olives, a small bottle of olive oil and two bottle of local wine. Kate looked at Drew in shock. There, in a small vase, behind this culinary treat were Zinnias! "Are you serious? How did they know about the Zinnias!!?" Kate asked looking at Drew. "I wish I had thought of that, but this is pure fate here, my love!" How incredible!! Kate and Drew hugged tightly and then he gave her one of 'those' kisses. He lifted her right up off of her feet and swept her off to the bedroom that overlooked the garden and pool area. The king size bed was laden with a large fluffy down comforter and rich colorful pillows. It was a very rich looking room with dark wood features and light colorful accents. He laughed as laid her on the bed. "I think we are about to mess up this very beautiful bed ......" and they did.

Later, Kate laughed as she looked around the room, colored pillows were strewn about everywhere. She loved the mess they made as they reconfirmed their love for one another. It was late afternoon and both of them were hungry. They made up a tray, like she often did at home, of the treats left for them in the kitchen. Drew had opened the wine to let it breathe, grabbed some glasses, and brought them out by the pool. They sat in the plush lounge chairs and sipped the wine that made her think of home. The cheese was so good - she wondered how to buy that and bring it home. How would she ever find cheeses like this at home? If she could just scoop this whole area and experience up, she would. It was so homey without being overdone. Kate looked over at the man she loved. His head was leaned back, and his eyes were closed. He looked completely satisfied. Slowly getting up, Kate looked around, they were completely isolated from any neighbors. There were no other places around for miles. She had already had two glasses of wine with the other delectable treats and was feeling a bit brave. She walked over by the shallow end of the pool and slowly took off her clothes. Stepping onto the first step to test the temperature of the water, she slowly and as quietly as possible lowered herself into the water. Skinny dipping had been on her bucket list and here she was!!!! Drew heard the slight splashing and opened his eyes and with raised eyebrows and said, "Kate, you little stinker! This is on my bucket list!"

"It's on mine too!! Come on in handsome!" She said beckoning him with her movements. He said "No, actually watching you skinny dip is on my bucket list." But he stood and quickly shed his clothes as if they were on fire, ran and jumped into the deep end of the pool. His big splash took out her hair that she had managed to keep dry. She laughed hysterically and they played in the pool like kids. Racing each other from end to end. Doing cannon balls off the side of the pool to see who made the bigger splash, and of course a diving contest. They didn't care who 'won'. It was so fun to be playful and act like a kid for a while. Kate was grateful that as the sun went down to cast some shadows over the pool so it wasn't like being in a spotlight. She knew her age and she knew what her body looked like. Kate was sensitive like most women were about their wobbly bits and although she was in good shape, she had some wobbly bits that she would rather not have a bright light on. Drew was oblivious to this. He was in good shape too but, as you get older things succumb to the dreaded gravity. She felt so comfortable around Drew though and he always told her how beautiful she was with or without clothes. She laughed to herself wondering if he might need to get his vision checked. While floating on her back, the conversation she had with her dad earlier seemed a little strange. He told her he was selling the house and wasn't sure what to do after that. He talked a little about maybe moving up near her. She was fine with whatever he wanted to do. He once again reassured her that he was ok and to please, please not cut their trip short. The autopsy had come back, and it was as suspected, a massive stroke. At least she had not suffered, Kate thought. She had also talked to Addie about her moving in with Joe and things were getting settled in there. She felt like she was missing so much back home. Here in Italy, she and Drew could be in a bubble. But it was a necessary bubble. They needed to get to know one another better as adults and to talk and plan out what they wanted with the rest of their lives together. They had a lot of family meshing together now. It was time to go in and get ready to go into the village and get some dinner.

There was a beautiful Villa Bordoni in the Chianti area they were eating in. This 17th century Villa had been made into a hotel and restaurant. Because it was getting dark out, they took the car. Tomorrow they would rent

Vespas to visit wineries and do some touring. Pisa for sure!

What a beautiful and romantic Villa! Tiny white lights were everywhere, lighting up the surreal looking place. They opted for eating inside as the temperatures were cooling off, were greeted with much fanfare by the enthusiastic staff. A cracking fire in the large stone fireplace created a lovely ambiance. Small tables, with white tablecloths, and candles were strategically placed so they all were blessed with a view of the sculpted gardens which were also lit up by thousands of tiny white lights. They were seated by a very nice woman who spoke very good English. She brought them menus that, she told them, changed all the time because they used seasonal fruits and vegetables. Wanting to sample as many different dishes as possible, they started out with Marinated beef carpaccio, a very thinly sliced meat with a salad of dates, tomatoes and fresh Tropea onions. Drew got the smoked salmon and trout with cucumber spaghetti with horseradish yogurt. They shared everything and gave reviews on what they thought. Wine was paired with each course. Next, they ordered a tagliatelle and wild boar ragu and ricotta and spinach gnudi with truffle shavings and pecorino cheese sauce. Gnudi were similar to gnocchi but instead of a potato dumpling, it was a cheese dumpling. Lighter than the potato version. Drew laughed and reached out to take Kate's hand." Now, I know you! Your eyes are going to roll back in your head and you're going to make those noises that should only be heard in the privacy of your own home! In fact, I think I heard some of those noises earlier today!" Kate laughed but could feel herself blushing all the way into her neck. "Oh my gosh, Drew! You're right! I have to be careful! I'm glad you're here to keep me in check! What do you think of the wild boar mac and cheese? I love the cheese sauce, but the wild boar is a little gamey for me. I am obsessed with the Gnudi dish!"

"I love the wild boar pasta! I think it's amazing!" The dishes were not big and it was easy to just have a decent taste so you wouldn't get too full. They enjoyed conversation and wine while they waited for the next course. Drew was more of a meat and potato man so he ordered the rack of lamb in a pistachio crust sever with a smoked eggplant puree and a raisin Vin Santo sauce. Kate ordered a 'Cinta Senese', which is a slow cooked pork neck with a peach chutney with almonds in a chianti reduction. Both of these dishes were divine, and Kate started in with the noise and the eyes rolling back in her head until she felt Drew rub his thumb over her hand. "Ha ha ha, I was doing it again wasn't I? I'm sorry it's a terrible habit that I need to break!" Drew looked at her lovingly, thoroughly enjoying his own meal. "I just don't like sharing those intimate noises with other people. Plus, they might be wondering what is going on under this table!"

"Oh, my goodness! I never thought of that! That thought right there might be the cure for me!" It was a lovely meal and they had not eaten everything on their plates to leave room for dessert. They were going to share a Millefolie. It was a crusty, delicate pastry with layers of vanilla custard and topped with fresh raspberry and pistachios. It was to die for! So light and creamy, you could taste the fresh vanilla in the creamy custard. "Kate, the day after tomorrow, I have signed you up for a cooking class here! It's starts at 3:30 and you get to learn how to make fresh pasta and create your own meal. I'll be here, too, but maybe off walking in the gardens. When you are done, we get to eat your creation! Surprise!!!" He said as they walked out to the car on the sky filled with glittering stars.

Really?! Oh, Drew, this is a dream come true!! I am so excited - thank you!!!" Kate had a surprise of her own. She had decided for Drew to have a lesson from Italian racecar driver, Luigi Fagioli. There was a track about 30 minutes away. She thought this was the perfect time to tell him because it was the same day as her cooking lesson. "Drew I have a surprise for you too, Luigi Fagioli, the Italian racecar driver is going to give you a lesson. It's the same afternoon as my cooking lesson!"

"Really? Luigi Fagioli!! Wow, he is awesome!! That's so nice of you!" Drew said swooping her into a kiss. The thing that really worked with Kate and Drew was that they really listened to each other. He would hear of her hopes and dreams, likes, and dislikes and then try, if he could make them happen. Even if it was something simple like her favorite kind of tea. Likewise, she loved to do special things for him to show him that she was listening to his needs, wants, dreams, likes, dislikes and how much she truly loved him. He was always doing such nice things for her and was the most thoughtful person she had ever met.

Chapter 12

The days seemed to tick by like hot tar going uphill. Peter thought he would lose his mind somedays waiting for his son to get back from Italy so he could finally meet him. He had spoken with Marsha several times on the phone. She is in no position to do anything. He could have her arrested. She was a criminal, a kidnapper. The others in the evil crime were dead. It was hard for Peter to even feel sad anymore about Evelyn being gone. He had spoken with his buddy, Charlie, about this many times. Charlie was no professional, but he thought Pete needed to see one. Otherwise, what happened to him, could eat him from the inside out and he hated to see it happen to Peter. Peter said no that he would not go to a counselor. He was so ashamed of what his wife had done, he was too embarrassed to tell anyone. How could he have been so stupid not to have noticed his wife was having twins? He put at least some of the blame on himself having been so naïve. He looked around the living room. The house was going on the market today, as is, furnished. If the new owners didn't want any of the stuff, they could throw it in the trash for all he cared. He had told Kate he was selling the house. Her only concern was where was he going to live. He still had no clue. But today was the last day he would be in this house of betrayal. Evelyn had always accused him of having affairs and he had never once stepped out on her. It wasn't that he wasn't tempted now and then, but he took his vows seriously. Even though she offered almost no affection, he still remained faithful. He had called and made an appointment with the Pastor of his church. They had all been very supportive after Evelyn had died. But the only one who knew the truth was Charlie and he had kept his word and told no one. He took one last look around the house, memories flooded his heart of Kate as a little girl. Running around and playing with her dolls, her fake kitchen with the fake food, and the stern looks she would get from her mother when Peter would get down on the floor and play with her. He needed to get out of here. He had put what things he wanted, from the house and garage, into storage. It wasn't much, some tools, photos, fishing gear and other odd bits. He walked to his car, seeing the **FOR-SALE** sign in his yard, he backed out of the driveway and he hoped he never saw this place again. Looking at his watch, he saw that he had just enough time to get to the church for his appointment.

Peter laid himself bare in front of the Pastor he had known for 30 years. He told him everything, from start to finish, while Ted listened without interruption. Peter wept bitter tears. tears that came from a soul that was crushed. Ted sat next to him in the twin chairs he had set up. From time to time, he would put a supportive hand on his shoulder while he wept. When he was done, the Pastor got up and opened his door, calling to his secretary to bring in two coffees. He handed Peter a box of tissues. There was a knock at the door and his secretary appeared with two steaming mugs of coffee on a tray with some sugar cookies. He thanked her and walked back over, setting the tray on the table in front of himself and Peter. "Peter, in no world, would I tell you that forgiveness is easy; it's not. What was done to you is terrible and we will never know why Evelyn did this terrible thing. I am not a counselor so I cannot give you a professional opinion, but as your Pastor who has known you for 30 years, I am going to do my best to give you good advice." He walked over and grabbed a book off the shelf of his vast library. "This book is by Dr. Charles Swindoll, we both know him, we have done many of his Bible studies here, it helps one to not only forgive, but to go on to have full, meaningful lives through a Christ centered joy of living through serving, sharing, and resting. **You** have a choice set before you, Peter. We all do. I am asking you to choose life. IF you stay in this dark place your heart will darken and die. You are not that man. You have said you have newfound relationships in your grandchildren. Let them be the reason for now. God will help you to heal your broken heart and use your suffering for His Glory. I have seen it many times in my life. Terrible tragedy can turn into something beautiful. If you like, we can meet regularly and go through the book together. There are also a few other books on grief that I can recommend. I would be happy to be alongside you as you purge forward on your path to recovery, forgiveness, and healing. You're not alone, my friend. Let me pray for you." The Pastor laid his hand on Peter's back and prayed for him. Peter wept once again, letting the betrayal and pain of not knowing his son fall onto his pants leg soaking in like cement. As Pastor Ted prayed, he could feel a lightening in his spirit. He could feel light, and love penetrate the darkest parts of his pain. The light searing the thick tar of scars and breaking them apart. When the Pastor was done praying, he told him he had felt the Holy Spirit in him. Pastor Ted handed him the coffee and they sat for a few moments enjoying the refreshments. He was going to come back every week and do what the Pastor recommended. Wow, he thought, as he walked out of the church office, I can actually feel that my burden is lighter. It felt so good. Like the darkness that had been weighing him down was being lifted. Like streams of sunlight coming through the clouds, he began to see things differently, he had hope! He had missed seeing his son grow up but now he had the opportunity to get to know him! Kate would know her brother! He was going to be a great grandfather! He had a future! He decided, then and there, that he was going to be happy no matter what! He got to his car and put his head on the steering wheel. He thanked God over and over again for his family, his dear friends, and for the message the Pastor had given him today. He thanked God for lightening his darkened heart. It never occurred to him that it was a choice. Stay in the mire or choose to get out. He was GETTING OUT! He laughed out loud! He was not excited about his future. No matter how much time on Earth he had left, it was going to be amazing. He was going to delve into the book he got from the Pastor and read the other recommend books on grief. He drove to his hotel room and called Charlie and told him about his session with the Pastor. Charlie was so relieved; he had been so worried about the direction his buddy was going in. Charlie invited him over for dinner with his family and he gladly accepted. When Peter got back to his room that night, he stayed up late into the night reading the book the Pastor gave him. It opened his heart to many possibilities and from now on, it would become a mission of his to find out what his passion was and to do it. He somehow wanted to reach out to others but prayed about what that might be. For the first time in three weeks, he slept soundly and restfully. A man's heart, finally at peace.

∞∞∞∞∞∞∞∞∞∞∞∞∞∞∞∞∞∞∞∞∞∞∞∞∞∞∞∞∞∞∞∞∞∞∞∞∞∞∞

Drew suggested they take the bicycles, that came with the villa, to town to the market to get some groceries so they could have some meals at the villa. Two weeks was a long time to have to go out to eat all the time and Kate loved to cook - *and* there was a great kitchen. It had been quite a few years since Kate had ridden a bike and she was not the most coordinated person, but she loved the idea of taking the bikes complete with the big wire baskets on the front. It was a beautiful morning and the trip to town was, maybe, a mile and a half. They had made coffee and had breakfast pastries that magically appeared every morning in a basket outside the villa door. She hoped to meet the people who rented it out at some point. Drew initially led the way on the narrow cobblestone street that went all the way into town. There were few cars that came down this way. Kate's competitive spirit kicked in and she stood up and pumped the pedals as fast as she could and sailed past Drew looking back and laughing at him. She didn't see the patch of pebbles that made their way on to the road and her tire hit them and the bike's front tire wobbled violently, she lost her balance and flew off the bike into the soft grass. The only thing that was hurt was her pride. The whole thing struck her as hilarious as she lay face down in the grass. She could only imagine how funny it looked from behind. She was laughing so hard her shoulders shook. Drew looked on in horror as he saw Kate fly off the bike into the grass. Oh no! Kate thought, she tried crossing her legs, but the deep laughter caused her to wet her pants. Oh my gosh!!! What am I going to do? Oh no, here comes Drew, but she still couldn't stop laughing. Drew came running up to her yelling "Kate, Kate are you alright? Are you hurt?" He saw her lying face down in the grass and he thought she was crying. He shoulders were shaking! Kneeling next to her, he heard the seam on the back of his shorts rip. "Drew, honey I'm fine! I am just laughing my fanny off and now to my horror and embarrassment I have wet my pants from laughing." Helping her off the ground, he looked and saw that yes, she had in fact wet her pants. "Well, I might be able to top that" and he turned around and showed her that the whole back of his shorts were ripped, and his underwear showed through. "Oh my gosh!! Aren't we the pair?" She said and bent over laughing again, he joined in the laughter as well and pretty soon they fell on the ground. "Another great story to add to our memories of Italy. Maybe we won't share this one?" Drew said. Just then a car slowly drove by them giving them odd looks, a middle-aged man pulled off to the side and said "Sei ferito? Hai bisogno di aiuto?" Drew assumed he was trying to find out if they were ok and so he stood up and gave the man a thumbs up and said "Sì, sì, siamo ok. Grazie." Kate looked at Drew impressed that he was learning some simple phrases. The only thing to do now was to ride back to the villa, change and then head back to town. As Drew got on his bike he said "Well, I guess my shorts are trying to tell me I need to start eating less food! I am so used to working out and being able to eat whatever I want. I should probably RUN to town! The shorts did feel a little snug this morning. Ha ha ha, I can't help it - it's just so funny!!" He said going off into another fit of laughter. At this point Kate's wet pants were getting uncomfortable and she needed to get out of them. She told Drew "I need to get out of these, I am soaked! " They made their way back to the villa, she got cleaned up and changed and he did the same. This time the trip to town went without incident. Kate loved the open markets! She now understood why Italians had small refrigerators. They ate mostly fresh food and she noticed that the custom here was to go to the market every day or so, to get the food necessary for the meals. They didn't use a lot of things that needed to be refrigerated. As they entered the small piazza in town, they saw a fountain in the middle. There were various carts of people selling fresh fruits and vegetables and a cart had fresh meat and cheeses hanging from hooks. There was a cart with fresh flowers as well. Kate and Drew went from cart to cart adding things to their baskets. There were no plastic bags. The meat was wrapped in the daily newspaper. Kate bought some fresh flowers, some things to make for dinner, and some beautiful fresh pane Toscano, and pane pugliese, a rustic sour dough. She also bought some beautiful Italian salami and shaved prosciutto cotto, she added some fresh greens, ripe red tomatoes, and some lovely cheese; she thought this feast would make great sandwiches. Her basket was full, and she saw Drew over by the fresh meat, so she joined him there as they tried to figure out what things were and what they would make for dinner. There was some spongy whitish stuff hanging and it looked really gross. She had no idea what it was, but she knew she didn't want to eat it. Drew leaned in and said "So, no sheep stomach then? "

"Oh my gosh, that what that is? Uh no, none for me thanks!" Kate took a step back looking all around her; she was in Italy, in a small village, buying food at an open market. The colors of this cornucopia were stunning. Her eyes trying to take it all in and put it in her memory. She took her camera out and tried to capture the feeling, but she knew she couldn't. Drew came up behind her and put his arm around her and said, "I know." After paying for all her purchases, she and Drew took their time getting back to their little Italian home.

This afternoon, they were renting Vespas and going to tour Florence and the towns nearby. Florence had many things to see, and once again, they had to pick out some top things on each of their wish lists. They would see The Galleria dell 'Accademia to see some of the works of Michelangelo, including the famous statue of David, then on to Ponte Vecchio to see the famous shops on the bridge, then finally off see the world-famous Palazzo Vecchio to see the 14th century architecture and clock tower. There was too much to see in a day! They drove to town in the car. They rented the Vespas and had a tour guide take them to the few places they wanted to go. They would be back before dark so they didn't have to worry. Their tour guide, Vincenzo, was a nice English-speaking young man with a great sense of humor. He first gave them some basic lessons on the Vespas and told them to follow behind and that it would take about 45 minutes to get there through the hilly wine country. It turned out better than either of them thought. It was another glorious day as the temperatures were in the mid 70's. The helmets were a little warm but that was ok. Kate thought about how her hair would be smashed when she took hers off. But she brought a clip along to put her hair up when they got to their first destination. The Galleria dell 'Accademia was incredible with many statues carved in marble by Michelangelo. Originally built in the 1700's, to give homage to the works of Michelangelo, it now included many paintings by Florentine artists of the Renaissance period between 1300-1600. Drew wasn't much into art history. He was blown away by the marble statues, but the paintings bored him. This trip was all about compromise and he was looking forward to the drive in the country to see, not only the landscape, but learn about making wine. He patiently walked behind Kate while she stood in front of paintings with her hands behind her back, studying some of the techniques of the artists. Luckily, they were on a schedule, and it was time to go to their next stop. Ponte Vecchio. This bridge was famous for its stunning gold jewelry but over time other venders had come as well. The bridge was unique in the fact that it was for foot traffic alone and lovers often strolled down its historic shop-filled street in the evenings. Called by Italians as the "passeggiata serale." Kate was not much of a jewelry person but got Addie, Jenna, and Jan some beautiful earrings. Drew offered to buy Kate something, but she declined gratefully. It was hard to maneuver the Vespas through the busy town but Kate loved it and was getting used to them. Drew said when he got back, he might get a motorcycle. Kate didn't like that idea at all. But for now, she would keep those thoughts to herself. Next, and last, on their list for the day was to go to Palazzo Vecchio to view the famous clock tower and Statues of David and Hercules by Michelangelo. Kate looked up at the famous statue and blushed. Gosh, she thought to herself, Michelangelo sure left nothing to the imagination! How did he carve out of marble? It was something to behold at 17 feet tall. Vincenzo had been a great tour guide, informative *and* funny. It was planned for them to stop at one of the many vineyards on the way home. It was now mid-afternoon and most of the shops were closing down. They had planned ahead of time to have an afternoon picnic in one of the olive groves on their way to the vineyard. They pulled off, went down a small narrow dirt road, and chose a spot that Vincenzo had pre picked out for them. It was near a small stream in the shade of some trees. They parked their Vespas and began getting the picnic set up. Kate had brought a large blanket for them all to share. She set out a variety of cheeses, olives, crunchy fresh panini, some sliced cotto salami, figs, fresh red crunchy grapes and, last but not least, a bottle of wine. She set everything out like a banquet. The men had gone off in different directions to explore a bit and to relieve themselves. Kate was glad she had gone to the bathroom before they left town. She walked over to the stream, washed her hands, took her little towel out and got it wet with the cool water then rubbed it over the back of her neck. She looked around and could not believe where she was once again. The whole experience was so unreal. She tipped her head back and thanked God as the sunshine touched her face and she drank in the light as it filled her spirit. Thoughts of home filled her mind, and it was hard not to worry. If she was being truthful, she was getting homesick. They had a week and a half left here. She reassured herself that soon they would be home - and to stay in the moment and enjoy this. This was the trip of a lifetime, and she might never be back. She heard the guys behind her laughing, and she shook herself out of her thoughts. "What's so funny?" She asked as she walked back to the blanket. "We were just laughing at how much food you have here. Did you invite 20 people?" Vincenzo said as he sat down on the large blanket. "Kate always likes to make sure there is enough food!" Said Drew, as he too, dropped to the blanket. Kate looked on in horror. "Oh NO!!!!" Kate said as she scrambled around her bag looking for something. "What is it my love?"

"I forgot to bring a wine bottle opener. Oh no! I forgot to bring glasses!" she said slapping her forehead. Vincenzo got up and went to his Vespa and search around until he came out with a small corkscrew. "I never leave home without one!" He said laughing and walking back to the blanket, he opened the wine. "But I am sorry to say I have no glasses. We will have to drink out of the bottle." They all had a good laugh about this, ate and drank the feast set before them. Vincenzo told them stories about his life and family. He had gone to the States for college and his family owned the vineyard they were going to today. He told them he loved doing these little Vespa tours so that he could keep up with his English. The vineyard, Fattoria di Lamole had been in their family for years. It was not large but very rustic and in a beautiful location on top of the hills. They had opened the house to visitors ten years ago to help pay for the life they wanted to keep. Drew had fallen asleep in the heat of the afternoon, and a belly full of good food and wine. Kate lay back as well and they all took a little siesta. Kate didn't know how tired she was until after the meal. They all rested for about two hours and then made their way to his family's vineyard. They drove up the winding narrow road to a charming hilltop rustic farmhouse. Bathed in the light of the afternoon sun, the front of the stone and stucco house glowed with the yellow washed surface. Reddish clay pots draped with pink Geraniums and purple Alyssum greeted them as they pulled up to the courtyard with a large Carob bush, a flowering bush native to Italy. At the base of the tree, a mini stone wall had been built in a circle around the tree and held many colorful flowers. Each window had a wood window box also filled with flowers. As soon as they pulled up, a tiny, gray-haired woman came running out. "Benvenuti a casa nostra Kate e Drew!" She said running up to them and bringing them in for a hug. Kate laughed and fell in love with the woman right away. Vincenzo laughed and his arms opened wide as he said "This is my Mama, Veronica. But everyone calls her Vera. Mama, I told you, you must speak English! I have been teaching her. We get many American, English-speaking tourists here."

"Yessa, my son teach me English. Welcome to ourrr home." She said with a thick Italian accent. She gathered them like chicks and brought them into the large kitchen. The kitchen had large wood beamed ceilings, a long white farm table with a huge fireplace. "Vera, I would like to speak some Italian, too, so we can help each other out." Kate said with a smile. She looked at all the dried herbs and garlic hanging at one end of the kitchen. Dried flowers brightened up the already bright white kitchen. What a homey atmosphere it created. Kate would definitely be growing her own herbs and drying flowers when she got home. She loved how it looked and how convenient it was for cooking. His mama had them sit at the table and she served them strong, rich expresso coffee in some beautiful hand painted demitasse cups. It was small but packed just the punch they all needed after their meal. Vincenzo disappeared for a few minutes and then came back and said the tour would start soon. He met them out front and invited them to join him on a golf cart. They drove around the hilly vineyard and saw row after row of terraced vine rows. The chianti grapes hanging almost ripe in the afternoon sun. The sunny warm afternoons and the cool evening helped create the unique flavor of this lovely red wine. At the base of the house, was a large rectangular swimming pool and an old stone and stucco bath house. Chairs were arranged around the pool and a pergola draped in blooming wisteria with a long wooden table laden with fresh fruits and flowers that looked like a post card she had seen that made her want to travel to Italy. Here she was! Again, Kate pinched herself to ensure this was not a dream. An older gentleman was walking down the path to the pergola with a tray of glasses and several bottles of wine. He waved them over to the table. "This is my father, Massimo. He will share with you our wines to taste." He said waving to his father. His father bowed to his guests and told them to please sit. "Siediti e goditi il frutto della nostra terra" His father said with a big smile. "My father says, sit, sit and enjoy the fruit of our land." Vincenzo then gave them a bit of history of the land, the grapes, and the production of the wine his family made. His father opened the wines and had them tasting with a glass to spit in after each tasting. His son had brought some lime sherbet to cleanse their pallets. The sun was setting, and it had been a long but perfect day. After thanking Vera and Massimo for the great tour and hospitality, Vincenzo gave them a fist full of lira making sure a large tip was included. He drove with them back to the small village where they dropped of their Vespas. They exchanged personal information and told Vincenzo he was welcome at their home in Minnesota, they also warned him not to come in the winter. He said he would love to visit some time and would contact them in the future. With final hugs, they took off in their little car and made it home just as it was getting dark. They were both exhausted from the day. Drew suggested they take a swim and relax for a bit. They didn't even talk about it this time, they just shed their clothes and dove into the deep end of the pool. They swam, kissed, talked about the adventures of the day, and floated until the stars came out. Kate got out, dried off and told Drew she would whip up a light meal for them. She put on a sundress, added a light sweater, and made her way to the kitchen where she chopped up fresh herbs, tomatoes, and cooked a chicken breast in olive oil and garlic. She took some pasta noodles and set them in the boiling water on top of the gas stove. Grabbing some Gorgonzola cheese, she got out a large hand painted pasta bowl and poured in the now cooked to perfection al dente noodles, she drizzled the top of the pasta with olive oil and added the fresh chopped herbs, chicken that she had cut into small pieces, fresh Roma tomatoes and topped it with the Gorgonzola cheese. She grabbed some ciabatta bread and set everything on a tray then brought it out by the pool and set in up on the table. Drew had flipped on the tiny white lights that were strewn everywhere making it look like a magical fairyland. She looked around for Drew, but he had quietly slipped in the house and changed. A few minutes later, he came out with one of the bottles of the wine they had purchased today and two glasses. They enjoyed a romantic dinner together. Holding hands, as they counted their blessings. Today had been amazing! After dinner, they got ready for bed. Tomorrow was to be another adventure. Drew was going to the racetrack for his lesson and Kate was going to the Villa Bordoni for her cooking class. Drew was going to need the car tomorrow, but Kate could ride the bicycle to her class. Drew would meet up with Kate later in the afternoon. For dinner tomorrow they would eat what she had learned to cook. Both yawning and happy, Kate fell asleep wrapped in her lover's arms. She slept so hard she didn't remember dreaming. They both woke up late in the morning, made love, and talked about the day ahead. While in the bathroom, Drew had made her a cup of English tea and served her one of the wonderful pastries that magically appeared at their doorstep each morning in a basket. The week was going by fast! They would be heading home one week from tomorrow. Kate felt the yearning of home again. But she knew when she got home, her head would be full of the memories she was making here. She was not done here yet.

Kate called Addie and it made her feel better knowing that the pregnancy was going well and that she and Joe were adjusting to living together. Addie told her mom that Grandpa seemed to be doing really well. Drew called his dad to check-in with him, , and was told that while they were terribly missed, all was well at the home front. Neal had gone to Kate's place to cut the grass and did some watering for her. Jan had been on house plant watering duty and general care of the house. So, Kate sighed, there is no need to rush home. She wasn't needed. Feeling a bit sad about this, she shared her thoughts with Drew. Drew reassured her that they wanted her to feel good about this trip. Not that she wasn't needed, but that they were "getting by" without her. Kissing Kate goodbye, Drew left, excited to have his day with Luigi Fagioli. Kate had a few hours before she needed to be at the Villa Bordoni for her class, so she went, got her book, and sat by the pool with a glass of fresh lemonade. She breathed in the scent of the flowers and took in the sight of the puffy white clouds. Getting warm, she slipped off her sundress and swam in the pool. As the time neared for her to leave, she made herself a quick sandwich. She then put on some light make-up, put her hair up, and put on a red sundress. She thought it best to wear some tennis shoes. This would be better on the bike than sandals. On the way out, she grabbed a light sweater for later in the evening, when Drew would join her for dinner.

Chapter 13

Peter paced back and forth in his hotel room. The house had sold for a good price and had only been on the market for three days. There had been multiple offers and he had chosen a family that had written him a letter expressing how they wanted to raise their five children in this area that had great schools, a park nearby that had a lake on it for the kids to swim in. The dad had said that he wanted to build a tree house in the big tree out back. Peter had met the young couple with the large family and the thought of children and laughter in this house, that held very little laughter, pleased him to no end. The only problem was, he had a house full of furniture to get through. His friend from church offered to have an estate sale for him and had stepped in and gotten all the details taken care of. Kate and Drew would be back a week from tomorrow, and he wanted all these details taken care of before she came home. In their last conversation Kate told him there was nothing she wanted from the house. She wanted him to make some money off the furnishings. He had not decided where to live yet. Jan had called him and asked if he would like to come to a welcome home party she was planning for Kate and Drew. She wanted it to be a surprise. He thought it was a great idea and asked if there was anything he could do to help out.

She told him just to bring himself next Sunday at 3pm at Neal's place. He had spoken to Marsha several times on the phone. His son would be home tomorrow from his band tour of Italy. Tom had been an Engineer at 3M for years and had taken a month off to tour with his band. He had been a drummer for years and been gigging on weekends for as long as he could remember. An Italian businessman had heard them one night in St. Paul and hired them on the spot for this once in a lifetime gig. He wanted Italians to fall in love with country music the way he had. He offered them a tidy sum and all expenses paid trip. Who could turn that down? After his divorce, he needed a new start on life, and this was just the thing he needed. There were no children to worry about. His wife and he had decided before they got married that they didn't want children. After 25 years, they had grown apart and amicably had parted ways a few years ago. Of course, Pete had gotten all this information about his son from Marsha. They needed to figure out the plan for telling him the truth. Marsha was fearful that once he found out, she would never see him again. She almost envied that Bud was dead and wouldn't have to face this. She was on her own. Why had Evelyn kept those letters? She had promised to burn them, and she had burned anything she had gotten from Evelyn. Water over the bridge she thought. The proverbial cat was out of the bag. Peter thought it best for the two of them to sit with him and just tell him everything from start to finish. He still had the diary and the letters. He worried that his son would reject him as well. But the man needed to know the truth. Next week, she would ask Tom to come for dinner to hear about his trip. When he got there, Peter would be there too. They both hoped for the best. Then, he would have to tell Kate that she had a brother and what her mother had done. It was a time of both hope and fear.

Jan called everyone in the family and told them of her plan for a surprise welcome home gathering at Neal's place next Sunday. There was a Vikings football game on as well and that helped Jan with what she would make for the meal. Chili, her famous corn bread, and her homemade chocolate brownies. This would feed a lot of people. She loved planning and giving parties, and with her large new family, she was so excited she could hardly contain herself. Neal thought this was very endearing and as they sat at the dining room table of her house, he helped her to get her thoughts organized and promised to help get everything set up. She counted in her head how many people: Neal and I, Drew and Kate, Addie and Joe, Jake and Jenna, Harry and Francesca, and Drew's son Sam would be here by then too. A welcome home for *him* too!! She was excited to meet Sam and had heard wonderful things about him. So, eleven in all. She thought about Neal's house and how she would set everything up. It was going to be October soon, and she wanted things to look nice. She had talked to Neal about bringing her

Fall decorations over to his place which, in a few months, would be her place as well. He told her to do whatever she wanted, and she was thrilled. She had bins of Fall decorations in the basement of her house and wanted to put her touches on his place. She had asked each couple to bring an appetizer, football snack or dessert of some kind. Neal had encouraged her to not do all of the food herself and that people loved to bring things, and everyone was happy to do it. Addie told Jan she was feeling really good, and that school was going really well. She told her that she and Joe were going to have a big wedding next June. How exciting for everyone! Weddings and babies! Jan was over the moon and told Addie to consider her as a grandma and that she was available to help. Addie laughed and said "Grandma! That is why I called you! I want to offer my help for *your* wedding!" She said laughing into the phone. "But, Addie, you are due on January 5th, right? You don't need to be helping me out at all! You have enough on your plate. Don't you worry about me, between the gals at church and Kate we will get this all taken care of, and we are just having a small wedding anyway. So, thank you but NO! I sure am missing your mom, gosh, I miss going over for coffee or tea in the morning. We would always have our morning chat and solve all the problems in the world over our breakfast." She said sighing into the phone.

"I know, when I have talked to Mom on the phone I haven't wanted to tell her how much I miss her. I can't wait to see her. I am sure she and Drew will have a lot of stories to tell. Plus, I always dreamed of having my mom put her hand on my tummy and feel her grandchild move. And who do I want to whine to about the joys of pregnancy? MOM! But I only have a week left and I am counting the days! How sweet of you to give them a welcome home party. I know they are getting in Saturday morning and will be tired with jet lag, but we all need to see them!!" With that being said, they said goodbye and said they would see each other next Sunday afternoon.

Neal had rented the apartment over the grocery store for Sam. He was coming home tomorrow and was going to run the grocery store for a while - at least for now. Sam wasn't sure what he wanted to do yet. Neal was able to get in the place and have some cleaners come in. He had bought some of the furniture he bought from Pete's to furnish the house. It worked out great! With two bedrooms and a bathroom, kitchen, and living room, and a stacker washed and dryer in a closet, it was perfect for a bachelor. Neal was very proud of his grandson for serving his country and wanted to welcome him to his new home. Jan had stocked the refrigerator with food and the cabinets with everything one needed to get started. She made up the beds with some new sheets and comforters, stocked the bathroom with towels, wash cloths, soaps and shampoo, toothbrushes, and toothpaste. She added some homey touches like candles and green plants. Neal had to stop her. "Ok, honey! I think we have done all we can do for now. I know you want it all to be perfect, but he is a grown man and will want to add his own stamp on this place. And thank you sweetie, you haven't even met him, and you are already being a grandma to him. That's one of the things I love about you is your thoughtful and generous heart. Sam will be so pleased! I didn't dare pick out a television for him. I am sure he wants a big screen because he is a big Vikings fan. Ok doll, let's go back to our place and let me make you some dinner." She gushed when he called it their place. For now, she was still living at her place next to Kate. She would not be moving in until she and Neal were married.

∞∞∞∞∞∞∞∞∞∞∞∞∞∞∞∞∞∞∞∞∞∞∞∞∞∞∞∞∞∞∞∞∞∞

The auction had gone better than Peter could have imagined. He had sold all the furniture! Neal had bought two-bedroom sets, the couch and lazy boy, coffee table, the small round kitchen table and chairs. He also had picked up some pots and pans and other tools for the kitchen. Harry had stopped over and picked out some of Peter's tools. Peter didn't want to take any money from his grandson but Harry put the money in his hand and said, "Take it, Grandpa." Peter had talked to Kates's friend Angie and had her looking for a small house up near the small-town Kate lived near. He had really liked it up there and enjoyed the company of Neal and Jan. They had told him about the great community they were part of. Peter thought it sounded great and had decided that he needed a fresh start. He didn't need much as it was just him. He was in good health and could still get around really well, but he wasn't sure about having a big yard to mow and a big house to keep clean. Angie assured him that she would find "just the right" home for him. She said she would get some places together and set up some showings for next week after Kate was home. A lot of people up here sold places before the winter. Angie knew of several people that were going to be moving South not wanting to endure the harsh winters any longer. There was a cute, little rambler, that was not right on, Goose Lake but across the dirt road. He would have lake access but it would not be right on the water. She thought this might be a really good fit for him. It was a small two bedroom with a bath and a half. There was only one level and everything he needed would be on one floor. Perfect for a man in his 70s. It had been well-kept and the couple moving out had done a lot of updates, so it was move-in ready. There was also a townhouse he might like and the apartment above the hardware store was available but that's where Grant had lived, and it was tiny and depressing. Peter admitted he was sick of living in a hotel. He had looked up pictures of the places Angie suggested online, and he was definitely leaning towards the little house a half mile from Neal's place. He called Neal and told him about the place. "No, it's not too close! I love that little house! They took great care of it, too! Great couple from our church too. They will be missed. Lots of folks up here snowbird in Texas but some just sell everything and move. I, for one, can't leave my grandkids. But there are days in the winter that I wish I didn't live here. But then May comes, and I forget those bad days. Good luck, Peter! And hey, Sam is thrilled with his new place and all the furnishings! That was perfect timing for both of us! See ya next Sunday!" With that said, they ended the conversation amicably.

∞∞∞∞∞∞∞∞∞∞∞∞∞∞∞∞∞∞∞∞∞∞∞∞∞∞∞∞∞∞∞∞∞∞∞∞∞

Kate was so excited about her cooking class! She was pretty good in the kitchen, but she was no Chef. She had good knife skills, so she had that in her favor. She was excited to see what the menu was going to be. There were two classes to choose from, and she chose the one called Cucina Povera. This was a rustic menu that used things from the region that was in season. So, depending on what time of year you were here, the menu would change. Kate had to stand up and pump the pedals to get her bicycle up the last hill to the beautiful Villa Bordoni. By the time she got up the hill, she was sweating and pooped. Great! She was going to be on her feet all day cooking and she was already hot and tired. A man in a white chef coat came out and greeted her. "Buon pomeriggio Miss Asher, sei pronta a cucinare?" Oh gosh - he was a nice-looking fella! But she only understood her name and that he said good afternoon. "Good afternoon, Chef! I hope you speak English!"

"Sì sì certo! But today you are Italian, and we will learn some good words for you. Va bene?"

"Yes Va bene." Kate said smiling. The Chef had her follow him back to the kitchen. The kitchen was all open and Kate saw that they had a Molteni range! This was the dream of every chef to have this kind of range. She knew she would never have one but what a thrill to be able to cook on one today.

"Ok first, we must wash hands and then you will be given to keep this apron to wear and take home. It has the family name of Bordoni on it. If you are good you won't stain it too much. Today we are going to make some rustic dishes loved by Italians everywhere. You take simple ingredients and put them together and you get a taste of Heaven. Today, we are going to teach you to make a rustic Polenta with sausage and caramelized onions, Lamb with Potatoes, and a Lemon Blueberry Mascarpone Ciambella, which is a classic Italian cake. You will learn technique, organization and how to pair wines with your meal. Ok! Kate, here you need to drink some water after your long trip up the hill on your bike." He said laughing and poured her a glass of cold water. The kitchen was spotless and stunning. He had set up a work area across from her and showed her how to get all the ingredients for the dish out and organized for the Polenta. She had never made it before and was eager to learn. Polenta was very versatile. He was impressed with her knife skills as she chopped the onion. She knew how to caramelize onions, but it was a thrill to do on the Molteni. Chef Enzo had her chop and brown some sausage and set it aside for the topping of the polenta. Kate likened making Polenta to cream of wheat. You had to keep stirring to keep the lumps out. The total cook time was about 30 minutes and she had to stir often. Hours passed as she learned many new skills in the kitchen. Enzo was a good (and handsome) teacher. Kate wondered how Drew was doing with his adventure. But she had to focus on the main dish of the Lamb and potatoes. Kate had never had lamb because it was LAMB! Who can eat lamb thinking of baby lambs? She had to push through it. Seasoning the lamb with salt and pepper, she set it aside, mimicking what Chef Enzo was doing. In a bowl, she added sliced potatoes, grown out back, cherry tomatoes cut in half, white wine, chopped red onion, a bay leaf, sprigs of rosemary, salt and pepper. They sipped wine while they cooked. Often, other staff members came into cheer Kate on, and it felt like she was with family. There was lots of laughing and joking around. One of them was Enzo's sister and she said she had to make sure her brother didn't get too big of a head. Enzo gave Kate a roasting pan and she took the seasoned lamb and added it to the bowl of the potato mixture. She tossed it, making sure all the pieces were adequately coated and then poured it into the roasting pan. Enzo showed her how to take a cheese grater and coat the top of the dish with Pecorino cheese and salt and pepper. This was to cook at 400 degrees for about 1 and ½ hours. Kate loved the part where staff would come in and clean up after the mess she had made. She needed one of those at home!! Next, they got started on the cake. Kate had to admit she was ready for a sit-down break. She asked Enzo if she could sit for a bit, and he led her out back to a shaded patio. She drank another glass of water and looked over the hills of the gardens. She checked her watch. It was 7 pm! Wow that went fast! Drew should be here soon! But she still had to make the cake and bake it. Dinner was set for 9 pm. It was hard to get used to eating this late. She didn't love going to bed with a belly full of food. Ok -back to work she thought, but she was having a glorious time! Back in the kitchen, Enzo had set everything up for the cake. It was to be baked in a Bundt pan. Kate was a good baker, and this was easy to follow. Enzo told her she had great skill in the kitchen and should consider going to cooking school. She laughed and told him she loved to cook as a hobby. Getting the cake in the oven, her eye caught Drew peeking in the kitchen. "Hey! How was your day? Are you going to have a new career as a racecar driver? "

"It was a blast! But no, I like to go fast but it was crazy!! How did your cooking class go? I see you have a very handsome chef. Do I need to worry that you will give it all up and move to Italy?" Kate walked over to Drew and pulled him in for a kiss. "You have nothing to worry about my love, but I'm not gonna lie, it was fun to work with a handsome chef. " Kate got cleaned up and Enzo had told them to go sit out under the pergola that was all lit up. There were several tables out there, and Kate and Drew, sat at a smaller table. There was a large family sitting at one of the long farm type tables and as Kate and Drew sipped their wine, they watched this rambunctious family interact. Seeing what looked like Grandma and her children and their children and a new baby, the conversation looked animated and filled with love and laughter. It caused a deep ache in Kate's chest, and she reached out and took Drews' hand. Once again the man could read her mind and said "I know honey, I'm homesick too. We just have a few days left and then we will be home with our family." Kate leaned in and put her head on his shoulder. They sipped wine while they waited for the meal that Kate had prepared to be served. First, came the creamy steamy Polenta topped with the caramelized onions and sausage, it was delicious. Next, came the lamb and she had to admit it was divine. The meal had the perfect ending with the Lemon/Blueberry Mascarpone Ciambella cake. It had been a wonderful day. After the meal, Drew took her bike and put it in the trunk of the car, and they made the short ride back to their little villa. They both slept like rocks. Tomorrow, they would ride horses on a tour of the Tuscany area and stop at two vineyards and have an afternoon lunch. Kate had not ridden a horse in long time, and she was a little scared and she told Drew and he said he hadn't ridden since he was a kid so they would be in on this together. As their time here waned they talked about what was left to do and both wanted to rent Vespas again to go and see the Leaning Tower of Pisa. The last few days they were in Italy would be bittersweet.

After getting a good night's sleep, they drove to Florence where they would meet up with the small group of people going on the horseback tour. Kate was helped up onto her horse and it seemed really high up. She nervously looked at Drew. The guide saw the look in her face and reassured her that the horses were tame and knew the trails well and not to worry. They met another couple from Canada and shared stories of their trip so far. It was another beautiful fall day in Italy and the temperature would be 80 degrees. What a beautiful day riding through the countryside, stopping in shaded olive groves for water breaks and a rest. In the afternoon, they stopped at a winery and had a lovely lunch and a short tour of the vineyard, tasting wines. The horses came with side pouches for purchases and Kate and Drew picked out several bottles of the local wine. They would not be able to bring them back, so they only got 2. The rest of the day was perfect and by late afternoon the tour was over. Kate and Drew drove home and reminisced about the day. Kate's bottom was a bit sore from the ride. Typical of Drew he complained about NOTHING! When they got back to the villa, Drew helped Kate put together a simple meal and they dinned outside by the pool. Kate shared her thoughts about everything going on back home. Drew was glad they had missed a lot of the drama. This is why he wanted to get Kate away for a month. They needed the break. He missed home too but not as much as her.

The sun streamed through the bedroom window and the warmth brought Kate out of her deep sleep. The first thing she noticed was the pain. Her whole body hurt. She got up, out of bed, and limped to the bathroom. Her legs felt like jelly and her leg muscles hurt so bad. The horseback riding! Owie! She filled the tub in the bathroom with water as hot as she could stand it and slowly lowered herself into the steaming healing waters. Oh, that felt so good. She lay back and soaked until the water started to cool off. She could hear Drew in the other room moaning himself. The soak had really helped and she toweled off and opened the bathroom door. Drew looked up with weary eyes. "Wow, I hurt in places I didn't know I had." He said slowly getting off the bed. "Drew, l know you are not a bath person but it really did help. Let me get the water running for you and take a soak while I make us some breakfast." He smiled and thanked her as he make his way to the bathroom. Kate dressed and went to the kitchen. It would be an Ibuprofen Day. She made some strong coffee. She opened the back door and picked up the daily basket of delights. She cut up some beautiful ripe melon and took her coffee outside to collect her thoughts and drink her coffee. Half an hour later, Drew came out with his coffee. "That really did help, Kate, thanks honey. I saw the Ibuprofen out and took some too. I think I am too old to ride a horse. It was great but I would not do that again. "

"I was thinking the same thing. There should be a warning for people before they do it! I mean everything was perfect about it but geez! I don't know about you, but I would like a day of rest."

"I'm so glad you said that because all I want to do is rest and maybe swim today."

"Sounds like the perfect plan to me. We can rest and figure out what to do next."

"I still want to do Pisa and rent the Vespas again. The was really fun."

"I know, and it didn't hurt so bad the next day".

Kate got up and set up a breakfast tray for them to enjoy outside in the beautiful garden. She lay back in the chair and let her senses fill with the smells, the sound of the birds, and the breeze gently moving through the pines. She was still sore but was glad they both agreed to have a down day. Drew said he was going to take a walk and stretch out his muscles. Kate got her book and read. It was fun to be in some of the places that her main character, Annah, had been to. She was almost done with the book series and would grieve her when it was over. They spent the afternoon lounging by the pool and soaking in the sun. They both knew that when they got back home, these warm temperatures would not be the same. It was Fall in Minnesota, beautiful, but not 80 degrees. They had a 10 pm flight on Friday night, so tomorrow was there last day in the villa. They would drive back to Rome Friday morning and return the rental car and take the train to the airport.

As if Italy knew they were leaving soon, they woke up to the sound of rain against the windows. Kate got up and looked outside. Thunder and lightning crashed through the hills and while she loved the rain, it would put a damper on the plans they had for the day. Drew leaned up on his elbow. Kate looked at him and sighed. His tan chest and the contrast of the white sheets nearly pushed her over the edge. He gave her a smoldering look and patted the empty place beside him. It didn't take long for her to get over to him and they spent the rest of the morning making the best of the bad weather. After refueling with food, they decided to take the car and go to Pisa. It was something they had to see. On the way they stopped at Baia a Cottibuono, a former Monastery, turned vineyard, culinary school, and a producer of excellent olive oil. Kate had wanted to purchase some of the oil to bring home. It was one of the tips they had gotten from the locals. The rain was steady but not heavy as they made their way to the City of Pisa. Driving to the Tower, they could see the tilt in the distance and wanted the touristy photo where it looked like you were helping to keep the tower from falling. On the way, Kate read out loud the history of the tower. Built in the 12th century, the structure began to lean from the soft ground and matters didn't get better when the bell tower was completed in the 14th century. At around 183 feet high, the height and weight did nothing to help the instability. In 1990, the degree of the tilt was at 5.5 degrees and was closed to the public while they worked on stabilizing the structure and by 2001 they had decreased the tilt to 3.97 degrees . Kate and Drew looked up at the beautiful tower. The details were stunning, they walked inside- fully intending to climb the 296 steps to the top. But after about ten steps, Kate turned and looked at Drew who was a few steps behind her. "Drew, I'm sorry, go on ahead without me. I'm too sore from yesterday."

" Oh, gosh Kate, I am so sore too! I cannot do it either." They moved off to the side to let other tourists by. Then made their way back to the car. Kate started laughing which got him laughing. "Moving forward, we are NEVER riding horses again! I say we go drink wine and eat yummy food on this rainy afternoon, for as we know, wine makes everything better!" Drew said as he started the car.

"Sounds like a great plan! Let's go!" They stopped at the village near their villa and spent the afternoon at a local trattoria and ate lovely food, drank too much wine, and had a lot of fun with the locals who called them "amanti dell'antichità" or ancient lovers. Every time Kate or Drew had to get up off the chair in the restaurant, they made painful noises which sent everyone into fits of laughter. But the more wine they had, the less noises they made. It was their last night here and it was bittersweet. How they had both fallen in love with this little village and they talked about maybe bringing the family over for a vacation here. But for a shorter time. Both woke up to the bright sunshine on Friday morning with fat heads from drinking so much wine. But there was packing to do, and they both moved slowly that morning. "I think we might have had a little too much fun last night, but I don't care! It was so fun! What a way to spend our last night in Italy." Kate said as she walked to the kitchen. Strong coffee was in order and Kate almost danced her way to the back door to pick up the basket of goodies. She would really miss this but also, looked forward to going to see Ashley at the bakery. It would be hard to leave all this beautiful food, but Kate knew now, how to use more rustic foods and bring them up to a higher level. She brought Drew a cup of coffee and handed it to him just as he was coming out of the shower, the towel tied low on his hips and his salt and pepper hair dripping, the water running down his chest in tiny streams. Those blue eyes and that body! She took the coffee out of his surprised hands and set it down and walked over to him and ripped the towel off of him and pushed him back onto the bed. He laughed sexily at her and let her have her way with him. She couldn't think of a better way to push through the morning wine head.

Chapter 14

Marsha had made a pot of coffee and nervously set out a tray with coffee, sugar, and cream, along with a cake she had made. Her son would be over soon. Peter sat across from her. There was nothing Marsha could do but pray. She was a kind and loving woman who had been caught up in a bad situation and because her heart was broken, from her inability to have a baby had made a terrible decision. Her husband Bud had felt the same. He loved children and the fact that Evelyn was giving them a baby made all the sense in the world....back then. Since he had passed away, Marsha would take the heat. She was very thankful that Peter would not press charges. She stood as she heard Thomas's car pull in and she walked quickly to the back door to greet her son. Peter stayed in the living room. "Hey Mom! It's sure good to be home! How are you? I have lots of photos to share and some gifts for you." He said setting some bags down on the kitchen counter. She hugged her son tightly and wondered if it would be the last time. "Tom, there is someone here to meet you and he has a story to tell you, can you come through to the living room?" She saw the confused and guarded look on his mother's face. What the heck was going on here? He thought but followed her to the living room where a tall, older gentleman stood up to greet him. He looked at the guy and thought maybe his mom had a boyfriend, which seemed unlikely but who else could it be? "Hi, Tom my name is Peter. Can you have a seat please? Your mother and I have some news for you." Marsha stood up and poured a mug of coffee for her son, adding a dash of cream and a few scoops of sugar, and handing it back said, "Would you like some cake too?"

Awkwardly, he took a plate with cake on it from his mom, Peter declined the cake but accepted a mug of black coffee. "Ok, you guys are freaking me out, what is this? Are you her boyfriend or something?" He said setting the plate of cake on the coffee table.

"Honey, no, he is not my boyfriend but we do have a story to tell you so if we can get started......" They had decided that his mom should tell him the story. Peter was a complete stranger to Tom. "Well, here goes..." Marsha should have been a writer, thought Peter, for she started at the beginning and went into minute detail of what the characters of the story were feeling and thinking. Tom's eyes filled with tears as he heard his mother tell of her many miscarriages and her broken heart that she and Bud would never have the kids they longed for. Tom had never heard of Peter and Evelyn, even though she was Marsha's cousin. But she went on telling the details of the story. His eyes almost popped out of his head when Marsha got to the part where Evelyn gave her baby boy to Marsha and Bud. Tom stood up taking a few deep breaths. "So, you're telling me that I am adopted. And this man right here is my biological father, and he had no knowledge of this?" He said looking Peter up and down. "Well, actually you were not actually legally adopted. We committed a crime. She gave you to us. No papers were ever signed. The doctor was in on our plan." She said walking over and running her hand down his arm. "Oh GOD!" He said shaking his head, "This is messed up! Where is this evil woman? Didn't have the guts to show up huh?"

"Tom, my wife, your....for lack of a better word.... mother..." He didn't get the words out before Tom shouted "She is NOT my MOTHER! She threw me away like trash!"

"Well, she is dead," said Peter without much feeling.

Sitting back down, Tom was shaking, and tried to take a sip of coffee. "Mom? I need something stronger than coffee," and Marsha ran to the kitchen and came back with a bottle of whiskey and poured three small glasses and passed them around. Tom sat there after slamming his shot of whiskey and said many bad words. After some time, Tom looked at Peter and said "It sounds like you were as much a victim as I was. Mom, I am not mad at you. Evelyn was going to get rid of me no matter what. At least, she gave me to you and Dad who have loved me more than a child could ever ask for." Marsha put her arms around his neck and wept while he stroked her arm and looked at Peter. "Tom, I would love to get to know you with whatever time I have left. You also have a sister named Kate. She is your twin.

She will be back from Italy in a few days, and she doesn't know about you at all. If you are open to it, I would love for you to meet her and for all of us to spend some time together."

"Italy? I just got back from Italy. I was touring there with my band. Wow, I have a sister! A twin!! I need some time to let all of this sink in. This is a lot!!" They all talked for the rest of the afternoon and together came up with a plan to talk to Kate. Peter said he wanted to talk to her alone. This was her mother that had done this terrible thing and she had passed away. It was going to be a lot for all of them. The two men agreed to meet for coffee with Peter's pastor. Tom was a man of deep faith as well and this made Peter very happy. The healing could begin.

∞∞∞∞∞∞∞∞∞∞∞∞∞∞∞∞∞∞∞∞∞∞∞∞∞∞∞∞∞∞∞∞∞∞∞∞∞

The flight back from Rome had been uneventful. They once again had first class tickets, thankfully because Drew had been a pilot. The fact that it was a night flight helped too. They were able to sleep on the plane and woke up to the sun streaming in the airplane windows. A light breakfast was served with fresh, hot coffee, fruit, and an omelet. After they were done with breakfast the flight attendant came by with hot wet towels. Kate pressed the towel to her face and let the steam take the grime from the flight away. She got up, went to the bathroom, brushed her teeth, and freshened up her make- up. The jet lag was going to be something. Her brain was thinking it was mid-afternoon, but it was almost 9 am Minnesota time. She had heard it took a week or so to catch up. She was so excited to go home! She couldn't wait to hug her daughter who by now no doubt was showing in her seventh month. Her baby bump had been pretty little when they had left a month ago. A MONTH!! It had gone by so fast! Kate leaned into Drew who looked so cute reading the newspaper with his reading glasses on. She wondered if she could talk him into being in the mile high club. Ha! She laughed to herself. Who was she? She better start reigning it back in! The airport was quite busy when they landed but all of their luggage had made it and it took about an hour to go through Customs. Kate was so irritated that when they searched her suitcase, they messed it all up. She had carefully packed things so it would all fit! The man at the airport had to shove things back in to get it closed. Her smaller suitcase held all her gifts and new clothes. She had carefully wrapped the olive oil and was pleased it made the long trip unscathed. Drew was quiet on the drive home. "I'm fine honey, just tired from traveling. I didn't sleep much on the plane, and did you know you snore?" He said laughing while he kept his eyes on the road. "I do NOT snore!"

"You most certainly do, Madam, but lucky for you it's cute!" Kate gave him a light tap on the arm and said,

"Oh YOU!" They finally pulled in the driveway of her home. Wow! The leaves were a plethora of colors! Reds, golds, and bright oranges. And against the deep blue sky -she felt like she was back in her little Heaven. "Wow! Look at this place! It looks stunning! Like the leaves are welcoming us home!" Drew said pulling right up to the back door of her home. "What a neat way see that, Drew!" They got out and hauled in their suitcases. There was a magical smell coming from a crockpot on the counter with a note.

WELCOME HOME, LOVE BIRDS!

CHICKEN DIVAN IN THE CROCK

WELCOME HOME PARTY AT NEAL'S

TOMORROW AT 2PM

LOVE, NEAL, AND JAN

"Oh, how sweet! Man, that chicken smells DEVINE!!!" Drew said laughing. That was really sweet! How thoughtful of Jan to think of them. There wasn't a stick of fresh food left in the house. Drew brought her bags upstairs and while she unpacked, she called and talked to her daughter. Drew could hear the squeals of delight as the two women talked. He called his dad and they spoke for a while about the trip and that they were home safe. Kate went to her closet and pulled out gift bags and tissue paper and began to separate the gifts she had gotten for people. She pulled out the new clothes she had gotten, and the two pairs of beautiful handmade Italian shoes. She sniffed the shoes and took in the leather smell. She carefully put them in her closet. She sat on the bed after finishing her unpacking and stared out the window. She had to shake her head a bit. It was surreal to be back her when yesterday morning she and Drew had woken up for their last day in Italy. Kate could hear Drew down in the kitchen wondering what he was up to. He was going to stay here with her tonight. The thought that he would go back to his place at his dads tomorrow filled her with grief. They had not picked out a wedding date yet. There had been too much going on. Kate called her dad quickly to let him know they were home. He was so happy to hear her voice and said he would be at the party tomorrow and couldn't wait for a hug. He assured her he was doing ok and in fact, wanted her to go and look at some places up in her neck of the woods to live. She was thrilled. Ending the call, she padded down the stairs. Drew had opened a bottle of wine and was sitting out in the screened porch. It was only 2pm their time but 8pm Rome time. He thoughtfully had grabbed two glasses. She opened the door and went to snuggle on the porch with him. They sipped wine and watched the afternoon boaters fishing and taking every last minute to enjoy the lake before it froze. They watched as geese flew in V formation, sand hill cranes making their ancient dinosaur like noises, large white swans swam past the dock. They sat in companionable silence. She patted

155

his chest and said "Drew, that was the most wonderful time I've ever had in my life. For me, it was our honeymoon. I am so deeply in love with you! You're my life, my soul, thank you so much for all you did to make all my dreams come true."

"Katie, my love, we are truly kindred spirits. I passionately love you and cherish every moment with you. You made all of my dreams come true! Now, let's get married! I don't want to spend another night without you!"

"Drew! I would love to just have a little ceremony too!! Let's do it soon!!! Tomorrow we can tell the family! Oh Honey! I agree! There is no reason to wait any longer". She said and they leapt up off the couch and held each other and jumped up and down like kids. "Ow, ow-ow," they both said laughing and then sat down. It was going to take some time to get over those damn horses. They ate the yummy dinner left lovingly for them at 5pm. For them it felt like it was eleven at night on Italian time, so they were tired. But they were told to try and acclimate as quickly as possible, and it would help with the jet lag. Drew fell asleep on the couch after dinner and Kate made it until 8. Both of them woke up at 3 in the morning. They had decided to get married at the courthouse as soon as they could get a license. Drew went online and filled out the paperwork and printed it out. Monday morning, they would go file and see when they could get in. Kate took this time to sort out her closet. She wanted to make room for Drew's things, and she had a huge closet. She pulled all of her summer clothes and shoes out and brought it all to one of the spare bedrooms on the main floor. She unpacked his suitcase and then made piles of laundry to do, sorting out by color and fabric. Drew helped her carry things down and they glanced at each other and giggled. "It's happening!!" Drew said as he sat on the bed in the spare room. "Woman! You sure have a lot of shoes! Is this just sandals?"

"Yeah, I do have a lot of sandals. But I keep them for a long time. I probably should go through them, but I just can't seem to part with any. Good thing there is another closet for me to put stuff in." Kate said as she organized the shoes in the spare room closet. As the sun came up, Drew had made himself a pot of coffee and Kate her English tea. The grocery store opened at 7 am and she needed to get some fresh food in the house. Drew wanted to go with her and see his son, Sam, who had gotten out the military last week. Kate loved that she would finally meet Sam! She had heard so much about him. He had joined the military at 21 and spent the last ten years serving his country. They made the short four-mile drive to the store and drove past the bakery where her friend Ashley worked. As the last-minute, Drew made a U-turn in the middle of the empty street and pulled up in front of the bakery. He was hungry and he knew Kate was dying to see her friend. The car had barely come to a stop, and she jumped out and ran in the sweet-smelling shop. She knew Drew wanted to see his son, so she ran up and both women screamed at the same time and they hugged and swayed back and forth. "Ashely! I missed you! We must have a girl's night and catch up on everything!"

"Oh Kate! I can't wait to hear about your trip and what is this?" She said pulling up Kate's left hand. Drew, stood back with a smile on his face watching the women. He was ogling the pastry case and Kate saw that he was drooling. "Yes! I have the most wonderful story to tell you about that! Let's see if we can get together on Tuesday and I'll tell you all about it! We need to get some food in our house but for now we need a little something, so we don't go grocery shopping with empty bellies."

"Congratulations you two! I'm so happy for you both! And to think it all started in my little bakery with you making your weird noises and Drew forgetting his jacket." She ran around to the back of the pastry case, and they picked out their favorites. "It's on the house today love birds!" She gave them each steaming cups of coffee to go with their morning treats. With a last hug and promises to meet soon, they left the bakery. Drew pulled up and parked in the grocery store parking lot and ate his chocolate croissant with lightning speed. Kate licked the remainder of her almond Danish off her lips and took several sips of coffee to wash the deliciousness down. Drew grabbed Kates's hand as they entered the grocery store and while she grabbed a cart he ran around the store looking for Sam. A clerk told him that Sam didn't work until noon. Disappointed, he came back to the cart, and they spent the next half hour getting things to restock the fresh food for their home." I'm sorry honey!" Kate said as they unloaded the bags into the truck of her car. "Don't worry about it! I'm going to come back after we unload the groceries. He lives in the apartment above the store."

"Oh, that's right! Okay well let's hurry home! After we get all this in the house you run along! I can put everything away. Do you want me to go with you?"

"Of course, I want him to meet you but maybe he and I could have some time alone first. I haven't seen him in a long time."

"That's just fine Drew, honey, come here." They met at the back of the car, and she held him tightly.

"Our new life together is going to be amazing, you're a wonderful man. Let's get this food home and then you can come see your son! I'm so excited for you!" With that, they drove the short trip back to her house. Drew backed up the car all the way to her back steps that led into her kitchen. Now, why had she never thought of that! She had always parked her car in the garage and then hauled the bags across the lawn. Life was better already with Drew! A few minutes later Drew ran out to his truck and sailed off into town to finally see his son.

Kate took all of the fresh food from the bags and put everything away. It was good to be home. She checked her e-mail and her publisher was bugging her about writing another book in her chipmunk series. That was good news! This was the first time Kate had been alone in a long time. Except for the day Drew had left early for his racecar lesson. It seemed strange. The phone on the counter buzzed and it was her dad calling. "Hi Dad, how are you doing?"

"I'm okay, I know I'm going to see you tomorrow, but I wanted to tell you that your mother's memorial service is next Saturday at our church at 11. We aren't going to do anything afterwards. Just a private service for the family."

Kate sighed, "It seems unreal to me. We will all be there of course. I'm sorry I wasn't here with you for all of this."

"Kate, I have the most wonderful friends and your kids have been amazing - helping me with the house and the auction. I'm pressing forward and am looking forward to looking at those two places with you on Wednesday. Is that day still okay with you?"

"Yeah Dad it's perfect. Why don't you come here first, and I'll make us some lunch and then we can go? Sound good?"

"Sounds good honey, thank you. See you tomorrow!"

Kate was so sleepy she went up and fell on the bed and instantly fell asleep. She woke up to the warmth of a body next to her and she rolled over and snuggled Drew's back. He was sleeping soundly. She quietly got up and went to the kitchen to make some dinner. She got out the ingredients to make Pasta and fagioli. A rustic, Italian dish. Kate got all the ingredients for the pasta dish out and lined it up next to her gas stove. In a large stock pot, Kate added her olive oil from the Monastery to the pot and cooked the chopped pancetta until the fat was rendered, next she added her chopped onions, carrots, garlic, and celery and cooked that until the onions were translucent. Next, she added about a cup of white wine and let the alcohol cook out of that. Pouring in the chicken broth next, and then salt, pepper, a can of chickpeas and a can of cannellini beans, lentils, a bay leaf, and some minced rosemary. The kitchen was starting to smell incredible, and her stomach growled. She brought this to a boil and then it needed to simmer for about half hour. She cleaned up her mess and then got some deep bowls out and set the table, adding some candles, water, and wine glasses. She cut up some crunchy fresh bread that she picked up from the grocery store and placed it in a wicker basket on the table. She searched the fridge and found the Parmesano Reggiano cheese and grated a pile of it next to the stove. She tasted the hearty soup, and the lentils were tender. Taking a cup of the soup she put it in her blender and made a puree. Then she added the little pastas to the pot and cooked them until done. Kate could hear Drew stirring upstairs. Perfect timing! She quickly added the puree to the soup and then added the cheese, stirring it in. It smelled like Italy! She grabbed the bowls off the table and filled them with the Heavenly comfort food and brought them back to the table. Bringing the cheese over to the table, she drizzled the top of the soup with a small amount of olive oil and more cheese. She lit the candles and poured the wine and the water. "Oh my gosh! What is that smell? You woke me out of a dead sleep! You evil woman!" Drew said coming into the kitchen and then stopped. Looking at all the love she had put into this meal, the table setting, the candles and wine......he felt humbled and blessed to be able soon call this woman his wife. "Kate, you darling girl! You know how to welcome me home. Thank you honey! It looks and smells wonderful!" He said and hugged her tightly. "I am the most blessed man in the world." He said while kissing the top of her head.

"Oh honey! You are too sweet, come let's eat! I'm excited to try this!"

It indeed was delicious! They took the crunchy bread and dipped it into the hearty soup. Yum, this would become a staple for the cold winter months ahead.

After dinner, Drew cleaned the dishes, He said it was part of the deal, she cooked, he cleaned. She wasn't going to fight him on that! He suggested they take the pontoon out for a quick "putt putt" around the lake. It was a beautiful evening, but it was getting cooler and they both grabbed jackets and headed down to the boat. They got back just as the sun was setting. The colorful leaves, the blue sky, and the reflection of them both on the water was a masterpiece. Kate looked up to the

Heavens and said to God, "Show off." Smiling and thanking God for her life and the everchanging masterpiece as the sun set. She thought of tomorrow and was so excited to see her family!

Driving up to Neal's house, Kate and Drew saw a lot of cars. Addie came running out with tears streaming down her face and hugged her mom. "Mom!!!! I missed you so much! You're really here!!" She said and then back away. Kate took her daughters hands and looked down at her every growing belly! She placed both her hands on her tummy. Just at that moment she felt her grandchild kick. "Oh, my goodness! You are welcoming me home too, little one!" Harry came rushing out and hugged his mom. Francesca was there behind him and hugged Kate as well. Her son, Jake, was next to hug her and then Jenna was right behind him waiting her turn. Joe and her father were just coming down from the house with Neal and Jan and they all took their turns hugging the couple. Kate brought her dad in for a long, tight hug. He held her back and looked into her eyes. They held both joy and grief. Last but not least a tall handsome man with green eyes stood before her. She looked way up for he was very tall." So, you must be Sam! Hello, I'm Kate! It's so nice to finally meet you!" He brought her in for a big bear hug. "Hi Ma! It's great to finally meet the woman who put a smile back on my dad's face! Welcome to the family." They all made their way back up to the balcony. Jan was delighted to see her friend Kate and they hugged many times. Drew gave Kate a special look and they stood together and Drew said, "Family, first of all thank you for this. It's so wonderful to have all our family together. Kate and I want to let you know that we are engaged!" The crowd roared with cheers! "But that's not all! We are getting married on Friday at the courthouse and you are all invited. Then, we are going to Franco's for dinner. We know it's last minute, but we don't want to wait and we don't need a big wedding. Please join us!" Everyone cheered and the joy was palpable. As the afternoon went on, Kate and Drew stood off to the side and watched their family. The guys were all in the living room around the large TV watching the Vikings game. The women were huddled on the deck chatting and Neal, Jan and her dad stood in the kitchen having some wine. What a wonderful day with family. Kate's heart felt full to bursting.

The next few days were very busy. Kate wanted a special dress for her wedding and she found the perfect blue dress. It showed off her curves but was modest at the same time. Drew had a beautiful blue suit that he would wear. He had picked up the license and made the reservation at the restaurant. Everyone was coming. What joy! Kate's dad was coming today for lunch and then they were going to look at the two places Angie had found for him. Last night Kate, Angie, and Ashley had met in town and they had a great girls' night. They had so much to catch up on. The girls were thrilled for her upcoming wedding. They had decided to make it a regular thing to meet on Tuesday nights for girls' night. Kate promised that next Tuesday she would have photos of Italy.

Kate heard the knock at her back door and was pleased to see her dad. "Come on in Dad!" She rushed over to him and hugged him tightly. She brought him into the house and had prepared a nice lunch. Sitting down across from him, he seemed.....she didn't know, nervous? He picked at his bacon lettuce and tomato sandwich and barely touched the soup. "Dad, what's wrong? Are you okay? Have you changed your mind about moving up here?" She asked inquisitively.

"Kate, there's something I have to tell you." He said taking her hand.

"Dad! Are you sick?" She asked with huge round eyes.

"No, I'm not sick, but you might get sick when I tell you.....it's about your mother....."

The End

Find out what happens in Book 4! Secrets, Brides and Babies on Cedarcrest Lake

Made in the USA
Columbia, SC
30 December 2021

53024041R00095